Borderland

'You see it?' she said. 'It's a Door. Can you guess what's on the other side?'

Zoë didn't hesitate. The space was so completely strange, so absolutely alien, that it could only be one thing.

'Another world,' she whispered and Laura smiled.

Zoë has always found it hard to make friends: her dad's job in the army has meant they have never stayed in one place for long. But now it seems that Laura really wants to be friends. Not only that, but she is letting Zoë into the big secret she has only shared with one other person—the Door into another world.

But once through into the strange, alien world of Shattershard, Zoë becomes uncertain of her feelings towards Laura and her brother Alex. What is their real motive for coming here? And why are they carrying books on modern warfare? As things escalate towards disaster, Zoë has to decide whose side she is on.

Rhiannon Lassiter was born in 1977. Her mother is also a writer and reviewed for several newspapers, ensuring that Rhiannon always had something to read. She began to read science fiction and fantasy when she was about nine years old and it is still her most enduring passion. She has always spent a lot of time reading and writing and even skipped classes at school to go to the library. The first novel she sent to a publisher wasn't accepted, but the positive feedback she received was a great boost to her confidence. Her first trilogy was published just after her nineteenth birthday, which meant combining her university degree with her writing. Rhiannon now lives in Oxford with two friends and two cats. *Borderland* is the first book in her new series *Rights of Passage*, and is her first novel for Oxford University Press.

Rights of Passage

Borderland

Rights of Passage

Borderland

Rhiannon Lassiter

OXFORD
UNIVERSITY PRESS

For Frances Hardinge, the fairy-godmother to this book

OXFORD
UNIVERSITY PRESS

Great Clarendon Street, Oxford OX2 6DP

Oxford University Press is a department of the University of Oxford.
It furthers the University's objective of excellence in research, scholarship,
and education by publishing worldwide in

Oxford New York

Auckland Bangkok Buenos Aires
Cape Town Chennai Dar es Salaam Delhi Hong Kong Istanbul
Karachi Kolkata Kuala Lumpur Madrid Melbourne Mexico City Mumbai
Nairobi São Paulo Shanghai Taipei Tokyo Toronto

Oxford is a registered trade mark of Oxford University Press
in the UK and in certain other countries

British Library Cataloguing in Publication Data available

ISBN 0 19 275237 5

1 3 5 7 9 10 8 6 4 2

Typeset by AFS Image Setters Ltd, Glasgow

Printed in Great Britain by
Cox & Wyman Ltd, Reading, Berkshire

Prelude

The Chamber of the Wheel is dominated by a circular table, in the surface of which is inlaid a spoked pattern of red on black. It is the one distinguishing feature in a room otherwise unremarkable. The shelves which circle the chamber hold regiments of black- and red-bound books each with a neatly stamped line of glyphs on the spine. In this region the symbol of the Wheel is a familiar image to those who traverse the book-lined corridors of the Great Library. It is used by the faction who claim this area as their own but the original significance of the Wheel is lost in obscurity.

In all the known worlds the Great Library is a thing apart. Inhabited solely by agents of the mysterious organization known as the Collegiate, it is said that even they do not know its true purposes or extent. Beyond this plain room lie hundreds of thousands more, all with the same book-lined walls, the same unassuming wooden furniture, the same open archways leading through more shelved corridors to more book-filled rooms. Papered with books and riddled with Doors, magical portals to other worlds, the Great Library holds more secrets than a lifetime of study could encompass.

This maze of knowledge is home to the Collegiate. Librarians, world-travellers, and magicians, the members of this secretive society have little in common other than the Great Library itself. Different areas of the collection are organized and indexed by various groups. The Wheel is a known force in the Collegiate; they have organized and catalogued their section and the Doors under their control, they maintain friendly relations with neighbouring factions, and they trade widely to obtain books which fall into their sphere of interest. But that sphere of interest extends wider than many realize, for the Wheel use their organizational skills not only in their area of the Great Library but in the worlds that can be reached through their Doors.

Tonight the faction's head council has met in state. The glossy surface of the round table gleams in the low lamplight and the book-filled shelves that stretch from floor to ceiling are cast into shadow. The councillors themselves are elderly and, like many Collegiate members, secretive and suspicious. Power is evident in their dry, measured statements and in the watchfulness of their hooded eyes. Since the Wheel is a large and potent faction there are hidden alliances here; plots and counter-plots abound as the meeting progresses with deliberate order.

'We come to the matter of the new Door,' Periphrast Diabasis, the secretary of the council, announces in a dry voice like a pen scratching across paper. 'The expansion along the new corridor was a success and we now possess access to a new world. Our agents have classed it as a Thaumaturgical Autocratic Mercantile Theocratic Imperium with Barbarous Marginals and a possible Rogue Element.'

All Collegiate members, of every faction, carry books. There is a susurration of sound as pages riffle and pens move smoothly, tracing the ciphers and glyphs of the councillors' codes and notations.

Golconda Moraine, a powerfully built man whose thick grey hair is still peppered with black, stirs abruptly in his seat, drawing the eyes of the rest of the council as he enquires abruptly, 'I have heard nothing of a Rogue Element. Why was this information withheld from the circulated agenda?'

'The agents have only recently returned from their initial assessment,' Periphrast explains without lifting his eyes from his own notes. 'I myself only received the full classification upon our arrival this evening.'

'Well and good then,' Golconda says in mollified tones. 'I beg the council's pardon for interrupting.'

Periphrast nods in acknowledgement. His eyes are disguised by the glass lenses set into his wire-framed spectacles and his voice as always is untroubled by any hint of emotion. Periphrast Diabasis has held the position of secretary of the Wheel's council for many years and is equal to any interruption or altercation among councillors.

'The new world is dominated by an Imperium cognominated the Tetrarchate. The Door opens near its capital city and our agents found information readily accessible to them. Through a succession of aggressive trade alliances and military actions the Tetrarchate has managed to bring the majority of the populated land under its sway. However, a state of conflict exists with certain Barbarous Marginals and here the agents advocate further study.'

'What progress has been made with the government?' a councillor asks and Periphrast flicks through his papers and replies:

'The Tetrarchate is powerful but their civilization is not advanced. With the right persuasion the government can be brought under our control.'

Another riffle of paper is overlaid with a few murmurs of satisfaction. The Wheel's aims and ambitions stretch far beyond this single world, but the idea of the Tetrarchate is catalogued neatly in their tidy minds among hundreds of similar instances and the expressions are thoughtful. Golconda Moraine is again the first to raise his voice.

'What of this Rogue Element then?' he enquires and, around the table, other councillors look up involuntarily or listen with pretended impassivity for Periphrast's answer.

'At the edges of Tetrarchate influence there are Borderlands. These are in the main inhospitable areas of desert or wasteland inhabited by Barbarous Marginal groups which attempt to maintain independence from Tetrarchate rule. Most of these are gradually being eradicated, but in one area they appear to be increasing in might.'

There are frowns on the faces of the councillors as they consider this. The Barbarous Marginals sit uncomfortably in their thoughts, a chaotic factor needing to be brought under control. All eyes are on Periphrast as he continues:

'The agents state that the inability of the Tetrarchate Imperium to quash these Barbarous Marginals is inexplicable by observed factors and suggest among a number of possible explanations the sponsorship of more adept Unknown Hostiles. A Rogue Element is postulated as potential sponsors.'

'That's fairly tenuous,' Golconda Moraine expostulates, raising his voice unnecessarily in his annoyance. 'There could be any number of reasons why these barbarians haven't been fully suppressed. The influence of a Rogue Element is an exceedingly unlikely scenario.'

From out of the shadows a thin figure leans forward from his seat, revealing the aged features of Vespertine

Chalcedony. The milky whiteness blurring his eyes betrays that he is half-blind and his claw-like hands tremble on the table, but his motion is greeted by a respectful hush. It was Vespertine who first discovered this section of the library, and who founded the Wheel faction when he persuaded others to take control of it. Now he speaks in a voice like the rustling of dead leaves.

'Unlikely, you think?' he rasps. 'I consider it unlikely that we haven't encountered opposition by now. Need I remind you that the rest of the Collegiate does not share our aims?'

'I only meant that the possibility is remote,' Golconda protests. But, as Vespertine's white-rheumed eyes focus on him, he subsides into his chair.

'We occupy a universe of infinite possibility,' Vespertine croaks. 'Each new world we control opens up more borders beyond which neither our knowledge nor our power extends. We must be alert on every front.'

Golconda Moraine bows his head in acceptance of the elderly councillor's argument and the secretary reels the rest of the councillors in with a smoothly interjected comment.

'Further study is called for,' Periphrast suggests and there are murmurs of support around the table. 'Shall we instruct our agents to return?'

There is a slight frisson of tension around the table, a suggestion of things left unsaid, before a questioning voice is raised.

'Are these the two siblings? They are very young.'

'They have certain specialities that make them valuable,' Vespertine answers. 'And like all the young they are power-hungry and ambitious.'

There are smiles around the table. All the councillors understand the secretary's words. They were all once young and arrogant when first initiated into the Collegiate;

they too have followed the smell of secrets, learning of the wheels within wheels in the organization that controls the catalogue of the worlds. The council of the Wheel comprehends a lust for power: it is what has brought them where they are.

'Before we decide to send them back I would see them for myself,' a councillor says and Vespertine nods his ancient head gently.

'By all means.' He spreads his hands in a gesture of openness. 'They await the summons of the council.'

When the council of the Wheel summons you it does not do to delay. Within moments two figures present themselves at the entrance of the chamber and bow their heads before the councillors.

'The reporting agents,' Periphrast announces and the councillors direct their shrewd stares at the new arrivals as he adds their names: 'Ciren and Charm.'

Oddities abound in the Collegiate. It is not to be expected that people from a wide variety of differing worlds will have much in common but Ciren and Charm are unusual even by the Wheel's standards. The boy and the girl who stand before the central table have identically composed expressions despite the august company of councillors. Both have the same white-blond hair, cut neatly to their shoulders, and both wear the same sober black. The obsidian arrowheads that hang around their necks identify them as Collegiate agents. The wheel symbols sewn onto the right shoulder of their tunics proclaim them agents of the Wheel. Twin pairs of violet eyes focus on Periphrast as they await instructions.

'The council have some questions for you concerning your report,' Periphrast informs them and Vespertine adds in avuncular tones, 'Did you find the new world congenial?'

'It is an interesting culture,' Ciren, the boy-twin, answers him. 'Trade and the arts flourish.'

'But the ruling government is riddled with internecine strife,' Charm, the girl-twin, adds. 'And the administrative and political apparatus lacks cohesion.'

'Nonetheless the military is effectively organized and well-armed. The citizenry is prosperous and complacent. At its current rate of expansion the Tetrarchate will soon be the sole government controlling the world.'

There is a murmur of satisfaction at Ciren's conclusion. As the councillors are well aware, a unified world government is easier to deal with than a hundred minor powers.

It is Golconda Moraine who finally, with an apologetic glance at Vespertine, asks the question that concerns the council the most.

'Your report makes mention of civil unrest at the borders of this Tetrarchate,' he says testingly. 'And you draw somewhat . . . surprising conclusions.'

The twins glance at each other as if deciding silently who should answer, then Charm fixes Golconda with her lambent purple eyes.

'Yes, councillor,' she says in a clear voice. 'The Tetrarchate has expanded to the point where it borders inhospitable areas inhabited by nomadic barbarians. However, until recently it appeared the situation was under the control of the local authorities.'

'What happened recently?' Vespertine asks in a thin, sharp voice and Ciren takes up the thread of the report.

'The nomads appear to have acquired military advantages ahead of their level of technical sophistication,' Ciren says simply. 'They must be receiving sponsorship from someone. Another Collegiate faction seems the most logical possibility.'

Glances are exchanged across the table and Golconda

Moraine's black brows are drawn into a ferocious scowl. Vespertine's hooded eyes study the inlaid surface of the table and across from him Periphrast Diabasis clears his throat, drawing all attention to him.

'Is it the decision of the council that Charm and Ciren should return through the Door and continue their investigation?' Periphrast enquires and agreement is unanimous.

'Then it is agreed,' Vespertine says, fixing the twins with his half-blind stare. 'You are now the Wheel's official presence on this world of the Tetrarchate and I expect you to take appropriate steps to investigate and nullify any threat to the Wheel. I presume you are familiar with our customary procedure in these cases?'

'Yes, councillor,' the twins chorus obediently and the other council members exchange glances across the table. The Wheel can be ruthless in its pursuit of order and there is no one here who doubts that the twins have been licensed to be the same.

But as they bow in obedience to the will of the council and depart to make the arrangements for their journey, both twins are thinking the same thing. Loyal as they are, there is one allegiance they hold more sacred than that to the Collegiate, the Wheel, or Vespertine Chalcedony. Charm and Ciren's highest loyalty is to each other.

1

The light was already going at three in the afternoon. Zoë stared out through the window across the wet tarmac of the playground to the group of parents clustered at the school gates. They were mothers mostly, some with babies in pushchairs. It was cold and blowy outside and mothers and babies were bundled up like Eskimos in smart autumn-coloured coats and hats and scarves. The babies kept throwing their hats and gloves and shoes out of the pushchairs and the mothers kept picking the things up and cramming them back on without pausing in their conversation.

Zoë could see three scenes layered blurrily in the window pane. Superimposed on the wet playground her own face swam palely out of the darkness, her expression strange and unfamiliar in the distorted light. On the surface of the glass the yellow-lit classroom was reflected full of kids heaping out piles of stuff from their desks and hurriedly packing bags with half a term's worth of possessions. Zoë's small rucksack was by her feet already packed. She didn't seem to have much more at the end of her first half term than she'd had at the beginning of it. Everyone else had bags and bags of loot; not just the endless books and files and papers and pencil cases but things they'd borrowed or swapped with each other only now being returned at the last moment.

Outside in the playground a flurry of little kids came out of the junior school building and swarmed around the mothers and pushchairs. She could hear their high-pitched voices floating across the playground as they waved lumpy clay models and pieces of cardboard with stuck-on macaroni. The mothers continued to talk over the heads of the little kids while they packed their belongings up into bags and hung them on the handles of the pushchairs. The babies waved their arms and legs like puffy starfish and threw all their gloves out again. Then, in a scurry of drifting leaves, the mothers began to walk off, little kids walking beside the pushchairs, as if the wind was blowing them away. Looking down at the little kid walking beside her, the last mother didn't notice her baby throwing his hat out of the pushchair for one final time as they walked off.

In the classroom behind Zoë a group of girls clustered together, discussing plans for the holidays and scribbling dates for parties in notebooks and on scraps of paper. At the other end of the classroom four boys were waving rulers like swords and duelling up and down the rows of desks. In the window Zoë's reflection watched them; an invisible observer superimposed on the group. After half a term here she didn't have the glamour of novelty or the acceptance of familiarity. Instead she was in a state she knew all too well: friendship limbo.

It didn't normally last this long. After eight different schools in six years Zoë was a past master in the art of making friends. You couldn't count on keeping friends after you moved, pen-palling never lasted; you had to make the time you spent somewhere matter. She was used to fitting in, to working out the complex network of friendships and cliques, and slotting herself into it. The trick was to blend in. Dress like everyone else and act like everyone else until you ended up accepted by default. But here things had been different. The trouble was that Weybridge was a small town; almost everyone else had come up from the junior school together, and in two months Zoë still hadn't found any way of fitting into the group. She'd ended up in the position she hated the most: sitting with the rejects and misfits and isolated from the normal community of social interaction.

A desk banged suddenly and Zoë half turned in her seat to see Morgan Michaels dumping the last of her books into a battered black haversack. Zoë looked away again quickly. She knew better than to try and make friends with someone like Morgan. She'd learnt to steer clear of the loners and the weird kids and Morgan, with her pitch-black hair and thick black mascara, definitely qualified as both. Being friends with Morgan would tar her with the same brush of social untouchability and Zoë didn't want to be an outsider. Instead her eyes automatically shifted away to Laura Harrell's desk right at the front of the room where Laura, a neat brown satchel at her feet, was bent over a book.

Zoë studied Laura sideways. While she had everyone else classified: rich kids, poor kids, social climbers and hopeless losers, sporty kids and brains, Laura was still an enigma. No one seemed to like her or hate her or feel strongly about her at all but Zoë had seen Laura talking to almost everyone at some point. The kids who smoked round the back of school at lunch, the popular group, the shy kids and the smart kids, the sixth formers who drove to school: everyone knew Laura. Without friends or enemies she seemed to drift through school; a solitary figure even when in the middle of a group.

A bell rang and the class fell back into a frenzy of last minute activity to finish clearing their desks by the end of registration. At the front of the room Laura tucked the flap into her book and put it into her satchel. Then she suddenly turned round in her chair and Zoë quickly looked away so that Laura would not catch her staring. To her right Morgan was fastening the buckles on her haversack, her long black hair falling over her face as she hunched down like a witch over a cauldron.

'Settle down now,' a voice called suddenly from the front and Zoë looked up to see that a teacher she didn't recognize had come in to take final registration. She read off the register quickly after dumping three piles of coloured leaflets on the front row of desks. The class surged towards the front of the room as they answered to their name, some of them taking the leaflets but most just heading out of the door when their names were called. Already Zoë could see streams of other classes coming out of the building and filling the playground and street.

Picking up her bag, Zoë stood up, letting the rest of the crush press past her in a flurry, while she waited at the side of the room. The teacher left as soon as she was finished, leaving Zoë one of the last in the classroom and, slinging her bag over one shoulder, she left the room. Outside the corridor was filled with kids packing up their lockers and crowding towards the double doors of the main entrance. Zoë ducked through the mass of people, heading left instead of right down the corridor. There was a side entrance this way which came out near the bike sheds and she had to thread her way past more kids unlocking their bikes as she came out into the grey playground. Then, just as she was about to turn the corner of the school building, raised voices stopped her.

'You're lying, Laura,' a voice said fiercely. Zoë froze and the voice continued, 'I thought you said you weren't going to interfere.'

'You're not listening to me, Morgan. You don't know the situation. I'm just trying to give you an idea of what's involved.'

Zoë recognized Laura's clear voice, speaking with the same calm tones as when she answered a question in class. Zoë hugged the side of the building, embarrassed to be overhearing the argument and not sure whether she had the nerve to just walk past them.

'I don't believe you.' A shadow moved and Morgan Michaels stepped out away from the side of the building. Zoë stared as her flying black figure ran off across the playground and then jumped as there was a jingle of bikes behind her. If she delayed any longer she would be seen hiding and, nerving herself, she walked quickly round the side of the building.

Laura was standing there. Her light green eyes were fixed on Morgan's back as the other girl disappeared into the crush of people at the school gates. Zoë uncomfortably edged past and set off across the grey playground, but with every step she felt Laura's green gaze boring into her back. It was with relief that she realized she had to run when she saw her bus was already standing at the front gates.

Throughout the long bus journey to the edge of Weybridge the light continued to fade and it was nearly dark by the time Zoë had got off the bus outside Weybridge Garrison: the army base. The guard on the gate looked at her pass without interest when she managed to find it at the bottom of her school bag, and waved her on down the gravel path that led to the rows of small white houses of 'Family Accommodation'.

Residence 4G was at the end of a row and Zoë let herself into the small house. Like all the others it was painted a neutral beige and carpeted in drab brown: no better and not much worse than most of the places she and her father had lived in. Weybridge Garrison maintained these houses for officers with families because of the lack of accommodation in the town itself. Yet another thing that set Zoë apart from her classmates but not something she was going to complain about. When her mother died her dad had offered her the choice of boarding school, living with her aunt's family in Yorkshire, or staying with him. Although moving schools all the time had its problems Zoë hadn't wanted to leave her dad.

Hanging her duffle coat neatly on a hook in the hall, Zoë carried her bag to her room. The house was silent; her dad was in Germany until the weekend, and Zoë turned on the stereo in her bedroom automatically as she dumped her rucksack on the floor. Like the rest of the house her room was plainly decorated except for an Omani throw on her bed and the small black and silver trunk in which she kept a few mementoes of the places she'd been. Dumping the school books out of her bag and on to her desk, Zoë turned to look at herself in the mirror.

Weybridge Grammar School didn't have a uniform but like most schools there was an unofficial uniform that kids tended to keep to. Dressed in dark blue jeans and a grey hooded top Zoë looked like most of the kids in her class. Her thick woolly auburn hair was scrunchied into a ponytail, leaving her face small and pale without its surrounding cloud. Zoë looked at herself and sighed. All term she'd dressed like this, doing nothing to stand out, and yet here she was at the beginning of the half-term holidays and without a single friend to phone and make plans with.

Automatically she thought of Laura Harrell. Laura didn't need to look like everyone else to fit in: she wore what she wanted. Zoë had secretly coveted her individual style. Laura made unusual clothes look cool and interesting. She dressed in swishing mirror-work and lace skirts, floppy-sleeved tops that buttoned or tied and a plum-coloured velvety jacket. Laura had coloured braids of embroidery thread woven into her long light-brown hair and a collection of bracelets that jingled from her wrists. If she was Laura's friend she could dress like that too, Zoë thought to herself, lying on her back on her bed. She and Laura would go shopping together in vintage clothes shops and maybe sometimes lend each other clothes. Everyone would be able to tell just looking at them that they were best friends.

Thinking of being friends with Laura reminded Zoë of how she had almost run into her around the back of the school. She wouldn't have expected that Laura and Morgan had two words to say to each other, let alone be having an argument in secret that had sounded pretty intense. Zoë couldn't help wondering what was going on there. It hadn't really sounded like the normal sort of friendship quarrel and she privately admitted to herself that she was glad. It would be too unfair if Morgan, with her weird black clothes and spooky eye make-up had been able to make friends with Laura.

'It's not as if it's hard to be weird,' Zoë said out loud. She'd met Goth kids before in other schools, especially the one in the States, and quietly despised them. They never seemed to care about having friends or being liked. They were just odd all the time; even when they were with other Goths they didn't so much seem to have friends as a kind of hive-mind of weirdness. When she was secure in a clique of friends Zoë had openly sneered at them, saying with the others 'get a life' when they acted strangely. Zoë had been deliberately avoiding Morgan all term because she wanted other people to see her as normal.

It hadn't worked though. Sitting up on the bed Zoë admitted that to herself. She'd been nice and normal all term, not making any waves, being friendly but not too cloying, hanging back at the edge of the playground waiting to be noticed or invited to join in. Now that the holidays were here she needed a different strategy. There weren't many kids her age on the base and she hadn't really bothered with them. But if she didn't want to spend the entire holidays watching TV or playing card games with her dad she'd have to find some way of impressing them.

Yanking open the door of her wardrobe, Zoë studied her clothes. Somewhere near the back was a patchwork wrap-around skirt and, stepping out of her jeans, Zoë changed into it. The weather was too cold to wear a skirt on its own and she put a pair of leggings on underneath and thick grey socks. Flipping rapidly through the hangers she tried to find an interesting top, finally settling on a striped one in different shades of purple that matched her skirt. Pulling the scrunchie out of her hair she brushed it out vigorously so that it fell back into its natural mass of thick curls. Looking at herself in the mirror she grinned fiercely: she looked almost like Laura Harrell.

The six neat rows of Family Accommodation were in the west corner of the base on the side furthest from the road. Residence 4G backed on to the fenced recreation ground that the kids were supposed to use. Normally the grassy rectangle was deserted, the base kids preferring to take the bus into Weybridge rather than make use of the set of swings or the lonely basketball hoop. But today when Zoë let herself out of the house she saw a few kids standing near the railings, clustered around the open bonnet of a beaten-up blue Volvo, and she headed towards them.

'Hey, Zoë,' one of them called, and Zoë recognized Dan Siefer. He was in Zoë's year but not her class or school and they sometimes sat together on the bus into town.

'Hi,' she said casually, joining Dan at the fence. 'Didn't see you after school.'

'My brother gave me a lift back,' Dan said, nodding his head towards the ancient Volvo. 'But then his car broke down.' He gestured at the three boys leaning over the bonnet, they were sixth formers Zoë vaguely recognized who also had parents who lived on-base. 'They're trying to fix it now.'

Zoë murmured something non-committal and leant back against the fence, watching while Dan's brother and his friends attempted to start the car.

'So are you doing anything tonight?' she asked eventually and Dan shrugged.

'There's a party on the edge of town,' he said. 'If Chris can get the car started we'll probably go to that.' He gave Zoë a brief sidelong look and then added a little awkwardly, 'Do you want to come with?'

'That would be great!' Zoë said quickly and then blushed a little at her own enthusiasm. 'I haven't really made many friends at school yet,' she admitted and Dan nodded.

'I get that,' he said. 'It's tough when you move around a lot.'

'Yeah,' Zoë agreed. 'Are you sure you don't mind me coming with you guys?'

'Sure,' Dan said casually and then called over to his brother, 'It's OK if Zoë comes tonight, isn't it?'

One of the boys looked up and waved at Zoë.

'Sure,' he said and Zoë smiled.

'I'll get my coat,' she said. She turned back to the house and Dan's brother grinned at her as she passed him.

'No hurry,' he advised. 'We'll be a while here yet.' He illustrated the thought by taking a battered packet of cigarettes out of his jeans pocket and passing them around as Zoë went back into the house.

It was evening by the time Dan's brother finally got his car fixed. There were five of them in the car including Zoë when they left the base and she had to budge up to fit in around a pile of paperback books that were lying on the back seat. Stacking them up on her lap she read a few of the titles and saw to her surprise that they were books about the army: basic training manuals, studies of guerrilla and terrorist warfare, and survival handbooks.

'What's this for?' she asked as Dan climbed into the back of the car beside her and his brother turned round in the driving seat to answer her.

'It's just stuff for Alex,' he said. 'The guy that's giving this party, you know? He wanted to borrow them.'

'What for?' Dan asked curiously as they pulled up by the exit barrier and he waved his pass at the guard.

His brother shrugged.

'How should I know?' he said. 'Maybe he wants to join the army.'

'Alex Harrell?' one of his friends laughed suddenly. 'Run it, more like. He's in my Politics class. He's got some kind of dictator complex.'

'Come on, Alex's all right,' Dan's brother protested but Zoë ignored him and turned to look at Dan.

'Is Alex Harrell giving the party?' she asked quietly.

'Yeah,' he said. 'Do you know him?' He looked surprised.

Zoë shook her head. 'No,' she said. 'But his sister's in my form. Laura.'

'Oh, right,' Dan said, losing interest. 'Yeah, I know Laura. She'll probably be there tonight.'

The barrier went up and the car swung out of the base and on to the road that ran round the edge of Weybridge. Staring out of the car windows Zoë saw the same triple layers of images as she had in the classroom that afternoon: the interior of the car, her own face, and the countryside slowly flowing past.

Zoë vaguely knew where Laura lived. She'd heard someone mention it at school. Bicken Hill was the smart area at the edge of Weybridge where all the really old houses were. It was right up against the woods that skirted the town: the Weywode Forest. As the car headed north Zoë wondered how many people in her class knew about this party; if Laura had invited them. Thinking about it she began to worry what they'd think if they saw her there. She didn't want to annoy Laura by gatecrashing a private party in her house. But when the Volvo turned into an unpaved side-road at the very top of Bicken Hill Zoë realized she hadn't needed to worry. The houses here were set apart from each other by some distance and Laura's was the very last on the edge of town. All down both sides of the road cars were parked and as Dan's brother found a space for the Volvo Zoë could hear the thumping beat of dancey-trance music coming from the garden of the house.

'Sounds like a good party,' Dan said, getting out of the car and unloading cases of beer from the back.

'Yeah,' Zoë agreed. Glancing at the pile of books she had been holding she added: 'Shall I carry these?'

'Cheers, Zoë,' Dan's brother said and she hefted them in her arms as they all went up the driveway together.

It was a massive party. Lights were strung on the trees

in the garden and people were dancing on the lawn or clustered in groups around a huge bonfire. Leaping shadows were thrown up against the trees and grey-white clouds gusted across the sky. As Zoë came round the side of the house she caught her breath; for a second the whole garden seemed magical and the people enchanted. Then Dan nudged her arm and she turned to look at him.

'Some party, huh?' he said grinning and his brother added, 'Let's find Alex so that Zoë can dump those books.'

They threaded their way through the partyers and Zoë looked around her thoughtfully. Most of the kids here were older than her, fifth and sixth formers and some even older still. Some of them looked as if they might be gatecrashers and she thought to herself that this was kind of a wild party for Laura's brother to be having and wondered what he was like. From what Dan's brother's friend had said Alex had some kind of dictator complex and she already knew that he was a school prefect and member of the inter-schools debating team. She'd seen him sometimes with Laura, noticeable for his height and long flapping trench-coat, and wondered about him.

Now, as she was thinking about him, she recognized him among the figures sitting by the bonfire and called out loud, 'Look, isn't that him?'

Dan's brother craned his neck to hear her over the music and, juggling the books awkwardly in her arms, she nodded her head in Alex's direction. As they made their way towards him Alex looked up and then waved with vague recognition as they joined him.

'Cool party,' Dan's brother said, dumping the case of beers he was carrying, and sitting down. 'Got those books you wanted, Alex.'

'Where do you want them?' Zoë asked, with a friendly smile, and Alex looked up at her in surprise. He had darker hair than Laura and it was curlier, falling to his shoulders in a mop not unlike Zoë's own, but his enigmatic smile was the same as his sister's.

'This is Zoë,' Dan's brother said. 'She lives out on the base with us.' He broke open the beers and handed one up to Zoë. 'Just drop them on him, if he's not going to take them, Zoë.'

'No need for that!' Alex said quickly and reached out to take the books. 'Cheers, Zoë,' he added affably and moved up on the tree trunk he was sitting on. 'Have a seat.'

'Thanks,' Zoë said and sat down, taking the beer as she did so.

Dan's brother and Alex fell easily into conversation and Zoë half-listened as she opened the beer can and stared into the glowing heart of the bonfire. They were talking about the military and Zoë was puzzled as to why Alex should sound so fascinated by the mundane details of military life. Maybe Dan's brother had been right when he suggested Alex might be intending to join the army; sometimes she'd met people like that who thought the military was like a great adventure. Zoë's dad was senior enough for her to know better. Being an army officer was a really tough job and being posted all over the world wasn't exciting as much as it was unnerving.

Zoë was feeling a bit uncomfortable about being at this party. Not only had she not really been invited but she wasn't sure her father would approve. Before she'd left the house she'd written a note for him. Even though he wasn't due back until the end of the weekend one of his early rules had been that even when he was away Zoë should leave a note on their message board if she was going somewhere. The one time she hadn't he had got back to find her gone and raised hell when she came home. But despite the note Zoë worried he wouldn't like this. She'd met lots of kids while she was moving around who smoked and drank and sometimes she'd joined them but she knew her dad wouldn't like it. He wasn't exactly strict but he'd explained to her that her behaviour reflected on him as a single parent and that if she started causing problems he'd have no option but to send her to live with her aunt.

Shaking her head, Zoë tried to dispel her doubts. This was the first party she'd been to since coming to Weybridge and her first real chance to meet people. Her dad had worried about how long it was taking her to make friends; he'd understand her reasons for coming. Relaxing she took a swig of her beer and looked around for someone to talk to. And saw Laura sitting only a couple of feet away and watching her from the shadows of the fire.

Zoë jumped and then covered her reaction with a quick smile and a wave.

'Hi, Laura,' she said, trying to seem natural. 'I didn't see you there.'

Laura looked at her gravely. She was wearing a light green dress that brought out her eyes and her long brown hair hung loose and wavy.

'Hello, Zoë,' she said. 'You look different.'

'I am different,' Zoë said recklessly. Her heart was beating faster and her hands were sweaty holding the beer can. It was uncanny how she'd come here by accident and found herself all of a sudden in the place she'd wanted to be all term: having a private conversation with Laura Harrell. She took another drink, feeling half-drunk already and suddenly liberated under the cover of the darkness and the relentless beat of the music.

'What do you mean?' Laura asked, leaning closer, and Zoë shrugged emphatically.

'Term's half over,' she said. 'And I'm tired of trying to fit in all the time.' She looked at Laura directly and added, 'I'm not as boring as you think I am.'

'I don't think anyone's boring,' Laura told her seriously. Then she smiled suddenly, the same enigmatic curve of the lips as Alex, as if sharing a secret with Zoë. 'But some people are more interesting than others.'

'Like Morgan Michaels?' Zoë asked and then blushed, wondering what she was thinking. But Laura had become suddenly still and was staring at her with something like amazement.

'What do you mean?' she asked quickly and Zoë looked away at the fire to cover her embarrassment.

'I heard you arguing today,' she said. 'I didn't realize you guys were friends.'

'If you listened for long you'd know we're not friends,' Laura replied, relaxing a little. But she was still focused directly on Zoë and she reached out a hand for the beer. 'Can I have some of that?' she asked and Zoë passed it over, watching curiously as Laura took a deep pull from the can and then wrinkled her nose.

'Ughh,' she said and smiled again at Zoë. 'I don't like beer much,' she confessed. 'But hardly anyone brought wine.' She stood up suddenly and reached down a hand to Zoë. 'I think there's some in the house though; do you want to go and look?'

'Sure!' Zoë said instantly, letting Laura pull her up and grinning at her spontaneously. 'This is a great party,' she added. 'I'm glad I gatecrashed!'

Laura blinked at her and then started laughing just as Zoë did, the two of them giggling together, even though Zoë wasn't sure exactly what the real joke was.

Heads turned around the fire and Alex stared at them with a strange expression on his face.

'Laura, what are you doing?' he asked.

'Getting something better to drink,' Laura told him casually and linked her arm with Zoë's. 'We'll see you in a bit, OK.'

'OK,' Alex said and added something else. But Laura had already swung Zoë around in the direction of the house and he had to repeat himself, raising his voice to call after them. 'Be careful!'

'What an odd thing to say,' Laura said and Zoë looked at the other girl, still not believing that they were walking together arm in arm.

'Is he over-protective, or something?'

'Not exactly,' Laura replied and shot her a sideways look that Zoë couldn't interpret. 'But he's strange.'

'So are you,' Zoë said boldly and Laura smiled.

'And so are you,' she returned. 'I'm only just realizing . . . ' She led Zoë into a darkened conservatory room at the back of the house and gestured towards a cane sofa while she rummaged among bottles on the table for wine. 'Who are you really, Zoë?' she asked seriously, coming back with the wine glasses to look down at her curiously. 'What are you like?'

It was like a dream, Zoë thought, as she sat with Laura in the conservatory, looking out into the darkened garden sloping up to the woods at the top of the hill. Feeling happy, if a little self-conscious, she answered Laura's questions readily. She'd never let herself boast about the places she'd been, knowing that there was nothing like vanity to lose you friends, but it was hard to resist Laura's obvious interest as she explained how she'd travelled with her father around the world.

'I changed schools a lot, you see,' she explained. 'And sometimes I had tutors when we weren't staying somewhere for long.'

'What's the most interesting place you've been?' Laura asked.

'Probably Saudi,' Zoë told her. 'We were there for nearly a year. Or America, but that wasn't as fun. Dad was there on secondment and there weren't many English

people there. The kids made fun of my accent at first.'
She remembered how mean they'd been until she'd
managed to fit in, learning to talk with the same twangy
drawl.

'Do you like moving around so much?' Laura asked
and Zoë thought about it.

'Mostly,' she said truthfully. 'Everything except making
friends. And losing them.' She looked away, wondering if
she'd said too much, and then asked nonchalantly, 'But
what about you, Laura? You haven't told me anything
about you.'

'About me,' Laura repeated, her green eyes distant as
she stared out through the windows and into the dark. Zoë
followed her gaze and saw, with a feeling of déjà vu, the
image she had been captivated by twice that day. Her face
and Laura's were reflected in the long windows of the
conservatory as phantoms overlaid on the mingled images
of inside and outside. Their eyes met in the glass and Zoë
saw Laura's expression change. 'Come on,' the other girl
said, standing.

'What?' Zoë got up automatically, feeling puzzled.

'Come on,' Laura said again. 'There's something . . . '
She hesitated. 'Just come with me, Zoë, if you really want
to know about me. It's easier to show you than to tell
you.'

Zoë put down her wine glass and followed Laura into
the night. The other girl led the way purposefully through
the half-wild garden and up to the end of the long lawn
where it bordered the edge of the forest. In the dim light
Zoë saw a small iron gate and watched silently as Laura
unbolted it and pushed it open, beckoning the way on to a
pathway through the trees.

'Where are we going?' Zoë asked and Laura hushed
her.

'Shhh,' she whispered, despite the pounding back-beat

of the stereo system. 'It's a secret.' Then she smiled and Zoë followed her example, grinning back with uneasy complicity as Laura closed the gate behind them.

The path led into the Weywode Forest proper and after only a few minutes the obscuring bulk of the trees had shut out most of the light and the sounds of the party behind them. Zoë had a brief qualm of anxiety but reminded herself that they were following a clear path and she could easily find her way back, just as Laura stepped right off the trail by a massive oak tree and turned back to mouth, 'This way.'

'Coming,' Zoë said softly and followed her.

She stepped carefully through the undergrowth, Laura's insistence on silence making her careful not to crunch too loudly through the fallen leaves. Laura was following some remembered path through the forest, not pausing at all as she led Zoë onwards and upwards. It was a surprise when she finally came to a halt in a small clearing and turned with a triumphant smile.

'This is it,' she said.

'What is?' Zoë looked around, puzzled.

'This place,' Laura said patiently. 'This is our secret. Only three of us know about it. Four now that you're here.'

'Know about what?' Zoë asked again and Laura stepped aside to show her what she hadn't seen before.

'This,' she said. 'The Door.'

Zoë looked and blinked. At first glance there was nothing exceptional about the pair of entwined trees. It was a common enough phenomenon. The lack of space among the clustered foliage had caused the branches of two trees to become entangled, forming a kind of archway at the edge of the clearing. Zoë glanced at Laura, wondering if she should suspect a practical joke, and then back at the trees. And saw it. A space where no space should be. In the natural archway the darkness was absolute. Nothing showed through, no leaves or undergrowth beyond it, no glimmer of light even though the rest of the clearing was just about visible. The archway was black in a way no natural thing should be and Zoë stared in fascination as Laura's voice spoke softly behind her.

'You see it?' she said. 'It's a Door. Can you guess what's on the other side?'

Zoë didn't hesitate. The space was so completely strange, so absolutely alien, that it could only be one thing.

'Another world,' she whispered and Laura smiled.

2

From the spear-point of a high tower the Archon of Shattershard surveyed the lands of which he was lord. Beyond the black rock ring of the fortress lay the endless shifting sands; the last rays of the setting sun stained the desert the colour of blood. Along the trade road the snaking line of the last of the trade caravans was being swallowed by the city, hastening to be inside the protection of the walls by nightfall.

Somewhere within that arid wasteland lurked the Hajhim, nomadic warriors concealed behind sand dunes and in gullies, ready to prey upon any merchant unwary enough to travel the desert by night.

'The desert is quiet,' Kal said out loud and beside him Cardinal Jagannath lowered his spyglass.

'The caravans have learnt to be cautious,' he said, replacing the spyglass in the folds of his crimson priestly robes.

'Too cautious.' Kal clenched his hands on the black

stone of the balcony. 'Every day there are fewer. Without trade our fortune will dry up like the sand. The desert is unforgiving.'

The priest fell silent and, when Kal looked to him for an answer, flicked his eyes at the Archon's honour guard: two soldiers assigned to watch after the boy-king at all times. Kal hesitated for a moment and then turned to say, 'Edren, Athen, wait outside the room, please.'

The soldiers bowed expressionlessly and returned into the tower room, stationing themselves on the other side of the outer doors and closing them. Out on the balcony overlooking the city Kal waited for the sound of the doors closing before speaking again.

'I've heard people are leaving the city,' he said.

'A few,' the cardinal admitted. 'Mostly parents with young children. They travel to stay with relatives and lock their houses behind them, take leaves of absence from their jobs. It's not a mass exodus, Lord Archon. People are cautious in these uncertain times.'

'If we lose the trade of the caravans they won't come back,' Kal said. 'Besides, how many of those people reached their relations safely? Do we know?'

'They travel together and some hire guards but it doesn't seem as if the Hajhim have any interest in attacking them. It's the merchant caravans they prey on.'

'The merchants come less often; the ordinary people are leaving,' Kal sighed. 'How long can the city survive?'

'Shattershard was mighty before the trade routes. The city itself cannot be taken,' Jagannath assured him but Kal shook his head.

'Our position is precarious,' he said. 'Here on the border we are caught between the Tetrarchate and the Hajhim. If I cannot ensure peace the Tetrarch will be displeased, perhaps enough so to have me removed as Archon.'

'Shattershard is independent of Tetrarchate rule, no matter how much we rely upon their trade,' the cardinal said smoothly. 'The people support you, my lord Archon, the Tetrarch knows that.'

'But without trade I risk losing their support. We cannot eat sand, Jagannath.'

Jagannath considered, studying Kal before he spoke. The Archon was new to his position, brought early to the throne by the sudden death of his father, and his slight figure was almost swamped by his heavy state robes. Jagannath, as head of the city's priesthood, had placed Shattershard's crown on Kal's head but it took more than a crown to make the boy an Archon.

'Where do your thoughts direct themselves, my lord Archon?' he asked curiously. 'These questions of state are new from you.'

Kal glanced up at the older man, his grey eyes thoughtful. Abruptly he turned and walked back into the tower room. Jagannath followed him inside, leaving open the doors to the cool desert night, and bowed as Kal poured a glass of wine and offered it to him.

'My thoughts are confused,' Kal admitted, pouring a glass of wine of his own and returning to the doorway, his gaze shifting over the towers and pinnacles of the city. 'My father was concerned about the Hajhi attacks but he believed he had the situation in hand. Now his ashes are flown on the wind and I do not have his confidence.'

'He was a wise ruler,' Jagannath said quietly. 'He expected to have many more years to instruct you. The illness that killed him could not have been predicted.'

'Could not?' Kal shrugged. 'It was not expected, his death is the show of that. What else does fate hold for us that we cannot predict?'

'An unanswerable question, Lord Archon.'

'And yet one that I must answer or else lose these

lands,' Kal said, raking back his blond hair from his face in an unconscious gesture of frustration. He looked again at Jagannath. 'You were my father's closest adviser, Cardinal. It was to you that he confided his most secret thoughts. He told me that he valued your counsel most highly. Advise me now how best to proceed.'

Jagannath shook his head, fixing Kal with an intent stare as he spoke slowly.

'My lord Archon, the priesthood will serve you faithfully until the end of your days but the decisions of government must be your own. You are young, it is true, and new come to your status. But your father taught you well. These decisions are not beyond your capability.'

The boy Archon bowed his head, accepting Jagannath's words, but continued after a moment.

'Tell me your thoughts, then. We are surrounded by several dangers. What think you truly of those who threaten us?'

Again the priest paused, taking time to arrange his thoughts, while Kal waited patiently, prepared to let Jagannath speak in his own time.

'My lord Archon,' he said eventually. 'My thoughts also tend to confusion. There is much here that is dark to me. There are the dangers we know of . . . the Hajhim . . . the Tetrarchate . . . but it seems to me that behind these there is something more, another force that threatens us. I cannot identify it but there are signs . . . ' He hesitated and Kal frowned.

'Signs? Portents? Does the priesthood predict danger unknown?'

'This doesn't come from the gods,' Jagannath said. 'It is no more than a feeling. There is something amiss in the world.'

'Can you explain further?' Kal's eyes were intent on the

adviser, taking him seriously enough to try to understand, and Jagannath tried to answer him.

'There is the matter of the Hajhim,' he began. 'They have grown bold but also they have grown cunning. They attack almost daily now, their ambuscades seemingly reckless and their numbers scarce, but their tactics have bested our own soldiers too many times now. I cannot understand it.'

'Yes,' Kal nodded. 'That is strange, truly.'

'Also the Tetrarchate,' Jagannath continued. 'I have friends in the capital who speak of corruption and chicanery at the highest levels of government. While the cities maintain an effective local government the Tetrarch himself is isolated and weak. This imbalance seems engineered. And even if it is not a strong faction might well make use of the opportunity.'

'Dangerous words, Cardinal,' Kal said thoughtfully.

'Dangerous times, my lord Archon.' Jagannath stared out into the night where the stars were now visible, strung out in complex patterns on the black sky.

He was silent for a long moment, Kal quiet beside him as they listened to the susurrations of the shifting sand, then finally concluded:

'My Archon, the world is a wide place. Who can tell what secrets it hides? Perhaps even the gods have puzzles to unlock. But I tell you truly I am afraid, because somewhere out there is a force which means us harm. More, I am ashamed for I cannot advise you against it.'

'You counsel wisely, Jagannath,' Kal said eventually. 'That your wisdom has not yet penetrated to the heart of this matter is no fault of yours. But we cannot let this lie. I will discover who my enemy is and, once unmasked, I will defeat him.'

*   *   *

As Kal and Jagannath left the tower top, returning to the Archon's palace by means of the twisting stairs cut into the rock face, a bell rang out sonorously, echoing and re-echoing from the pinnacles of Shattershard. The last dawdlers from the merchant caravan, casting anxious glances over their shoulders at the blackness of the desert, hastened to get their loads inside as the massive gates of rock began to swing shut.

Passing by in the other direction a group of shrouded figures were leaving the city, their sand-coloured robes swishing about them as they skirted the gate guards. No Hajhi was permitted to remain in Shattershard at night. The guards watched them narrowly but didn't challenge them as they departed. From beneath those flowing robes the handles of scimitars could be glimpsed and the guards had no wish to delay the closing of the gates.

As the last echoes of the bell faded, the gates swung shut with a tremendous boom, reverberating through the rock fortress, and the tribesmen were alone on the sandy rock road. Watched from the towers, they made their way down into the desert, speaking in low voices that could not carry across the sand. A few Hajhim were armed as warriors and walked alone, alert to the sounds of the desert. Some of the rest carried goods in baskets back from the market place. Others, with jobs as servants in the city, wore the livery of those they served. But one group didn't fit into an obvious category. Three merchant traders with a small donkey-load of goods walked alongside a woman with two young children and an elderly man carrying a battered old sword. A young warrior, whose face was hidden by a burnoose, a scimitar and curved dagger protruding from long sandy robes, strode along beside them.

'A good day's trading,' one of the merchants leading the donkey remarked to her neighbours. 'Our goods are in more demand now that the caravans are fewer.'

'Half of them are from the caravans anyway,' one of her companions pointed out and they laughed together. 'This way we get the profit!'

'Thank the war-bands then,' a boy with his hair in a warrior's plait said loudly, overhearing them. 'For taking the risk to gain those goods.'

'Without us to sell them what use would Tetrarchic luxuries be?' the woman with the donkey shot back. The rest of her group slowed to watch the confrontation, gazes shifting automatically to the slight figure of their hooded companion.

'There's nothing noble about selling muck to scum,' the warrior boy sneered. 'While we're fighting Tetrarchate soldiers you're selling jewellery to their wives.'

The old man laughed wheezingly at that and the boy shot a glance at him and met instead the flash of dark eyes as the hooded figure shook her burnoose back.

'All the Hajhim play a part in the fight against the Tetrarchate,' she said sharply, her right hand resting on her dagger. 'Who are you to judge which of us has the hardest work to do?'

'No one, Jhezra.' The warrior boy shook his head. 'I meant no disrespect.'

Jhezra shrugged, letting her hand drop from her weapon, and jerked her head dismissively.

'It's nothing,' she said. 'We're all on the same side. The stone city is strong but the sand is stronger.'

'The sand is strong,' the rest of the Hajhim who'd been listening said together. 'The desert has no mercy.'

'We still stand in the shadow of Shattershard's walls,' Jhezra said resuming her walk. 'Let us be silent while enemies watch.'

The Hajhim fell obediently silent, even the young warrior, taking their lead from Jhezra as they continued into the sand. Behind them torches burnt in the heights of the Shattershard towers but ahead the desert was dark. No one looked back, knowing from long experience at what point they would be out of the sight of guards or their spyglasses, letting their eyes adjust to the night.

The sand dunes deepened and the party of travellers moved quietly off the road at the next turning, their booted feet thrumming softly on the packed sand.

'Well met, travellers,' a voice whispered over the sand and Jhezra looked up to see a war-band on horseback emerge from the shadows of a rocky outcrop.

'Well met, warriors,' Jhezra replied, halting as the two groups exchanged quiet greetings and the rest of the walkers moved on further into the desert. 'How fare you?'

'We patrol,' the leader answered, dismounting. 'But the desert is quiet tonight. And you?'

'I was in the stone city,' Jhezra replied.

'Is that wise, honoured one? If the stone-dwellers knew who you were . . .'

'They know nothing of that.' Jhezra tossed her head. 'To them all the Hajhim look alike.' She curled her lip contemptuously. 'They are foolish and ignorant.'

'How goes it for them in the city?' the warrior asked curiously and Jhezra shrugged her shoulders carelessly.

'They are worried by the loss of so many caravans,' Jhezra said. 'Feeling runs high against the Hajhim. Even when the stone-dwellers buy from our people it is with fear and suspicion.'

'They are right to fear us,' the warrior said. 'Our day is coming.' He paused. 'Do you come with us on patrol?'

'My path lies deeper into the desert,' Jhezra told him. 'I must inspect the war-camp.'

The warrior bowed his head in acquiescence, swinging back on to his horse, and signalled to the rest of the war-band to move out. As they filed past the leader paused a moment longer, looking down at Jhezra to ask, 'Does Iskander come again soon?'

'I expect him daily,' Jhezra reassured him and the warrior nodded.

'Fare well then,' he said and rode off after the war-band.

The stars shone brightly as Jhezra made her way across the desert. She had no need to watch her path, the dunes were as familiar to her as the streets of Shattershard were to its citizens, but her eyes drifted over the silvery sands thoughtfully. Inside the city she felt trapped. Not so much by the high walls of black rock and the looming towers but by the endless crowds of people. The traders in the markets hectoring passers-by, bartering loudly, coins chinking as they made their deals; the house servants lugging goods up the steep twisting streets and sweeping dust from the courtyards; the chanting voices of the priests as they walked in procession along the roadways; it all set Jhezra's teeth on edge. In contrast the emptiness of the desert was as familiar and welcome as the night's cool breeze.

What was not so familiar was the respect the rest of the Hajhim were showing her. Two years ago Jhezra had been no one at all: just a scruffy Hajhi girl herding goats in a desert village. Now she was deferred to by almost everyone. Even seasoned warriors spoke to her with formality, for she had done what seemed impossible: she had come up with a plan to fight the Tetrarchate. It had been her life's ambition to earn herself a place among the war-bands and finally she had not only warriors' blades hanging from her belt but a senior role in the war-camp. It felt strange to be so respected. Pleasant but strange. Shaking her head, Jhezra tried to dispel her doubts. Without a doubt her life was better now; it had been ever since she'd met Iskander.

*   *   *

At night the temperature of the desert fell fast. None of the Hajhim risked travelling in the depth of night without an important reason. In all directions the desert lay quiet. To the east the rock-ring city of Shattershard still burnt lights in its towers and on the high bridges while citizens stayed up into the early hours of the morning. Further east a low scree of rock rose up gradually into the foothills of mountains, a road winding up through them towards the lands controlled by the Tetrarchate.

High up on the mountains a uniformed group of soldiers had set up camp just off the road. Dressed in blue and silver, they were obviously identifiable as Tetrarchic troops; their tents, the saddles of the horses, and their packs all in the same colours. The camp was laid out with military precision in rows of tents, the largest reserved for the commander of the troop. However, among them one anomaly spoiled the precision of their lines. A darker tent, made of a tightly-woven and almost oily-looking brown fabric stood among their ranks not far from the general's own tent.

The soldiers were going about their own business of watering the horses, preparing meals at the cook pots, staking down the tents, and setting a watch at the perimeter. But as they passed the small brown tent they paused for a couple of seconds to glance at its two owners sitting at their own fire just outside the entrance. More than one passer-by averted their eyes quickly, making a surreptitious gesture intended to ward away evil. Sitting quietly by their fire the two strangers paid no attention.

Dressed alike in plain black clothes and heavy winter cloaks, warm enough to keep out the mountain cold, at first glance they looked unprepossessing. But their faces were eerily identical. White-blond hair, chopped evenly to their shoulders, framed their dead-pale pointed faces dominated by huge dark purple eyes. Oblivious to the curious stares of the soldiers they talked in low voices: the girl sharpening a long knife with a whetstone, the boy hunched over a leather-bound book.

When the troops had finished setting up the camp site, Ciren finally put down his quill pen and closed the heavy volume.

'Anything important?' his twin asked, glancing up.

'Nothing very significant. Just some vague impressions,' Ciren said, passing across the book.

Charm leafed through it idly. Although the sections were written by the two of them alternately, the handwriting was the same, marching neatly across the vellum pages in calligraphic loops and swirls. The most recently written section was as her twin had described it: depictions of the scenery they had passed through, sketches of the blue and silver uniforms of the soldiers, and a rough map of the mountain passes.

'You're observant, young man,' a voice said from behind the twins and they turned simultaneously to fix their eyes on the troop leader. General Shirishath was conscious of a feeling of dizziness for a second as those purple-black stares regarded him expressionlessly. Then the girl-twin's lips spread slowly into a charming smile and he relaxed.

'General,' she said, standing politely, her brother mirroring the motion. 'You honour us with your company.'

'Thank you for permitting us to travel with you,' Ciren chimed in. 'Our letters of safe conduct have a lot more force when backed up by an entire division of Tetrarchate troops.'

Shirishath allowed himself a feeling of pride and bowed slightly acknowledging the compliment.

'Old soldiers learn to respect magic users,' he told the

twins. 'It never hurts to have a magician owe you a favour.' They joined in as he laughed and he nodded in the direction of his tent. 'Would the two of you care to join me for a cup of wine and perhaps resume our conversation of last night?'

'Our thanks, General,' Charm assured him, picking up her knives and sheathing them at her belt. 'We should like nothing better.' And the twins fell into step with Shirishath as he led the way to his tent.

The Hajhi war-camp was deep enough in the desert that Shattershard couldn't be seen. At first glance the sand dunes seemed to stretch uninterrupted into the distance but as Jhezra came nearer the shapes of tents arose out of a low dip in the land.

Like all the Hajhi camps it was a temporary arrangement. At one side of the camp animals were tethered: horses, goats, and hunting dogs. On the other side was the camp fire, protected from blowing sand by a ring of stones and a low canopy. The tents themselves were round and sand-coloured, shaped like upturned baskets over hoop-frames, and of varying sizes. Jhezra passed by unchallenged but she knew that her approach would have been spotted several times over by watchers concealed by the deceptive smooth curves of the dunes.

The warriors in camp were resting, mending harnesses and tack, sharpening blades or checking bow strings. Most sat outside their tents by small fires and cast stones in gambling games. From the big central fire came the smell of roasting goat and nearby, underneath a low canopy, the majority of the war-camp sat on heaped cushions and rugs, eating and drinking together. Jhezra stopped by the fire to cut a piece of meat and chewed it as she walked towards the rest of the warriors.

'Jhezra!' a voice called out and she glanced to her left to see Tzandrian striding towards her. 'How goes it?' he asked, offering her the flask he carried.

'It's good to be back,' Jhezra said, swallowing the last of the meat and taking a swig from the flask. The drink was hot and fiery and she grinned at Tzandrian as she passed it back. 'I always feel tense in the city.'

'Who can blame you?' Tzandrian shrugged, falling into step with her as they walked a little way off from the heat of the fire. 'They've grown soft and fat on the wealth of the Tetrarchate.'

Out on the sand were slowly moving figures and Jhezra and Tzandrian paused to watch them. Warriors armed with scimitar and sickle moved in silent combat, fighting their own shadows thrown across the pale sand by the firelight behind them. From the side so the warriors' shadows would not be disturbed, Jhezra and Tzandrian swapped the flask back and forth as they watched until finally one of the blade dancers noticed them. Stepping back from her shadow and saluting it she came over to them and took a deep swig from the flask as Jhezra offered it to her.

'Did you beat it, Vaysha?' Tzandrian teased and the girl laughed, sheathing her blades with satisfaction.

'Honours were equally divided,' she told them seriously before turning to Jhezra. 'I didn't know you were back. Is Iskander with you?'

'No.' Jhezra shook her head. 'Perhaps tomorrow.'

'When you see him, tell him I have finished the books he gave me,' Vaysha said. 'And that there are more that I want now.' She gestured vaguely towards the camp. 'I've made a list.'

'A list?' Tzandrian looked puzzled. 'What kind of list?'

Vaysha looked pityingly at him and explained:

'In each of the books there is a list at the end saying

what other books the writer has used as his sources. When I read a book that interests me I choose from that list what I want. Then Iskander sells it to me if he has it or sends away for it.'

'I can't see how you can learn anything about fighting from books,' Tzandrian said, unconvinced, and Vaysha's eyes gleamed.

'Come and test it then?' she said and Tzandrian reached for his blades instantly.

Jhezra laughed, accepting the flask back from Vaysha as the two warriors moved out on to the sand. As her friends traded feints with scimitar swords and sickle daggers she watched from the shadows, feeling relaxed at last. Sooner or later she would have to report on recent events in the city but for now she could rest in the security of the war-camp.

Ciren and Charm walked together through the mountain encampment. Although they were below the snow line it was still bitterly cold. Pulling their cloaks tight around themselves they walked past the sentries and stood together on an outcrop of rock. The sentries eyed them uneasily as they passed but didn't challenge them.

'You read Shirishath well,' Ciren said softly and Charm nodded. She didn't smile but her twin smiled for her.

As long as they could remember the twins had been together. Growing up in the Collegiate as apprentices to Vespertine Chalcedony and then as agents for the Wheel, they'd learnt to use their unusual magical powers in tandem. When Charm smiled she could read minds and when Ciren was in a silent trance he could feel the presence of magic. In combination their talents were more than enough to see them safely across this world. Shirishath was just one of many Tetrarchate officials whose minds Charm had plundered of their secrets and by now the twins knew more about this world than most people who lived here.

'Look,' Ciren said, pointing into the distance.

In the thin light of star-shine they could make out the expanse of the desert shining palely ahead, sand dunes rippling like the waves of a vast ocean. On the near edge the low rocky foothills of the mountains came to a straggling halt beside the black upthrust of the city of Shattershard. The black peak stood on its own, its centre blasted away by unknown force to form the shape of a great cauldron, the hollow inside forming an impregnable fortress.

'Shattershard,' Charm confirmed. 'Do you believe that we will find the answers we seek here?'

'It is the source of the conflict,' Ciren reminded her. 'In disturbed areas Doors are most common.'

'Now that we are almost at the city do you sense anything?' Charm asked. 'If there's a rogue Collegiate element around here they must surely be coming through a Door.'

'There's power here.' Ciren's expression was distant as he concentrated, using his own unique talent to sense the vibrations of magic in the atmosphere. 'The city is full of different magics. Local conjurings and ritual magics with a scattering of stronger powers. A few talents scattered across the desert but the power is unfocused.'

'What about Doors?' Charm asked quietly and Ciren closed his eyes, concentrating.

Charm waited, her own expression blank and her mouth slanted into the slightest of smiles, while Ciren was in his trance. Although she didn't have Ciren's power to sense magical signatures, her own abilities enabled her to drop into rapport with his mind as he searched, feeling him concentrate as if listening to faraway music.

'It's there,' he said eventually, breaking out of trance.

'A Door?' Charm asked.

'More than one.' Ciren met her surprised eyes and nodded. 'I can sense two. One a little way outside the city. Another . . . ' he paused, 'another somehow underneath it.'

'More than one?' Charm looked surprised. 'All this time we've been postulating the existence of a Door out here as a very unlikely chance. Now suddenly there seem to be two?'

'I know.' Ciren shrugged a shoulder. 'What can I say? These things happen. Caravaggion of Mandarel wrote of a world with a ring of ten Doors in a circle and none anywhere else on the world at all.'

'I hadn't read that.' Charm looked intrigued. 'What was the result?'

'According to Caravaggion the local barbarians built a temple complex in the area and worshipped the travellers as gods for a couple of centuries before deciding to try going through the Doors themselves. Caravaggion is descended from them.'

'I should remember to read the appendices more,' Charm said and Ciren laughed softly.

Looking out across the desert the girl-twin furrowed her forehead, thinking about the ramifications of what Ciren had sensed.

'How do two Doors affect our hypothesis?' she asked. 'Could there be more than one rogue element?'

'That seems fantastic.' Ciren thought for a moment. 'I'm inclining towards the point of view that we could be looking at Uninitiated World Travellers as patrons for these Barbarous Marginals. Perhaps there's no real danger here after all.'

'Interesting,' Charm replied. 'Unfortunately, I doubt the local situation is likely to be improved by the introduction of these Tetrarchic troops we're riding with.' She jerked her head at the ordered rows of tents behind them. 'The real question is how advanced have these marginals . . . ' she paused for a second.

'The Hajhim,' Ciren interposed and Charm nodded.

'How advanced have they become?' she wondered out loud. 'It doesn't matter immediately who's responsible for their recent successes. Are they strong enough to defeat the Tetrarchate here at Shattershard?'

'If world-travellers are responsible it may be easier to defuse the situation,' Ciren pointed out. 'People who've been jumping about between worlds are generally responsive to the idea that there's an organization dedicated to their interests. If we can get them to swear the oath, the local situation may resolve itself.'

'You're a pacifist, Ciren,' Charm said, staring out across the desert. 'You reason elegantly but people are unpredictable. Everyone has their own interests and ambitions. Everyone has their own world view. ''When Doors appear, interests clash.'' Dalandran the Itinerant said that.'

'According to Caravaggion, ''Conflicts are resolved by communication or domination''.'

Charm quirked an eyebrow.

'If there is such a person,' she said lightly. 'I'm beginning to suspect you invented him.'

Ciren smiled and then the twins were silent for a while, relaxed in each other's company as their minds pursued divergent trains of thought.

'If it is world-travellers who don't know about the Collegiate, what should we plan?' Ciren asked and Charm hesitated for only an instant.

'We're sworn to tell all world-travellers about the Collegiate,' she said. 'As for our particular faction and interests, that we can leave until we see what the situation is. I'd be inclined to suggest we look into those Doors first to get an idea of where any Outside Influence might be coming from.'

'Agreed,' Ciren said instantly. 'But I'd add that it's necessary to take soundings about the local situation to see how close it is to flashpoint. If the area's already in conflict there's the potential that it could be subject to rapid escalation.'

'You're right,' Charm agreed. 'And you'd better spend more time with your bow than the book for a while. If there's going to be a battle here we need to be prepared.'

'If there's going to be a battle here we had better recite the litany of Doors tonight,' Ciren said and Charm raised her eyebrows.

'If we're not word perfect on our list by now I'd be surprised,' she said. 'We're ready for this, Ciren. Let's meet it without panicking ourselves with extra preparation.'

When Jagannath returned to the temple Kal walked slowly back to the court rooms of the palace. Carved into the black rock of Shattershard, the Archon's palace was a maze of staircases. Some wound up towers in tight corkscrews, others curved grandly around the side of reception rooms and audience chambers, still more were staggered from balconies to galleries or from room to room in an almost imperceptible slope. But although the outermost towers and turrets of the palace had spectacular views of the inside of Shattershard the bulk of the structure was burrowed deep into the rock walls and Kal's own rooms were far inside the mountain.

Now he passed through the function rooms wearily. It was late at night and the court had retired for the evening. The mage-lights hanging in the staircases glowed dimly as he made his way towards his rooms. Edren and Athen followed behind him at a steady pace and Kal tried to ignore their watchful presence. The two soldiers had once been his friends. Before his father's illness they had trained together, hunted together, and spent their hours off duty and out of lessons in the city together. When his father started to get ill Kal had been told to choose bodyguards from the ranks of his friends and he'd chosen Edren and Athen because he trusted them. Now he felt he hardly knew them. When they'd all been at lessons together it had hardly mattered that he was the son of the Archon. All the students had their own talents and some had aristocratic, clerical, wealthy, or magical connections. Since his father died everything had become different.

When Kal reached his rooms he nodded to his guards and Edren and Athen stationed themselves outside the door as he went inside. He changed clothes automatically, shivering a little in the cold of the room. It was too late to light a fire but, shrugging into a thick woollen robe, he poured himself a glass of black wine from the pitcher standing near the fireplace. It had been heated earlier by a servant and the thick liquid still held a lingering warmth and the alcohol soothed his worries.

Six months since his father's death and the task didn't seem to get any easier. In only a few days his life had been changed out of all recognition. Now, instead of spending his time studying with tutors and sword-masters, he was occupied in meetings with councillors and inspections of the city guard. His father's advisers were constantly telling him how to be Archon but Kal increasingly felt that the Hajhim were out there somewhere taking lessons in how to overthrow borderland cities.

He couldn't remember when he'd last spent an evening with friends or in a tavern or listening to music or reading a book that wasn't about politics or government. Most evenings involved hours of putting in an appearance at court, listening to the various claims of advisers, and listening to the general gossip of the city's most powerful. When he returned to his rooms it was mostly too late to do anything more than drink a glass of wine and fall asleep. More and more he was finding he needed it just so he could sleep, or else he tossed and turned through the night, startled from fitful dreams into fearful imaginings of the future.

Kal's investiture as Archon had been hasty by necessity. When his father's sudden illness had ended his reign the people of Shattershard had been uncertain of the future. The aristocracy, priesthood, merchants, and magicians had been unanimous in confirming Kaddith's only son Kal as Archon in his father's stead. But increasingly it seemed as if the mountain city would be lost unless a way was found to combat the increasingly hostile Hajhim. Kal knew all too well that if the city could not stand on its own the Tetrarchate would send troops to defend it against the desert nomads and that would signal the end of any independence for Shattershard. Once you accepted the Tetrarchate's protection any independence you claimed for yourself was at an end.

Kal's crowning had been a city holiday and the crowds had assembled in thousands to cheer him as he rode in procession to the cathedral, hundreds more bowing before the altar as Cardinal Jagannath declared him Archon of Shattershard. The event had been designed to reassure the citizens that the city was still safe in the hands of the local government and for a time they had been convinced. But Kal knew he had not lived up to the promise of that day. The Hajhim still threatened the caravans, trade had slowed to a trickle, people were thinking of leaving the city, and the Tetrarch sent messages of displeasure from the capital and was threatening to send an experienced general to stamp out the Hajhim. Now Jagannath was suspicious of secret enemies. Kal felt a hundred years old instead of sixteen but without any of the wisdom age was supposed to bring.

Finishing the last of his wine, he resisted the temptation to pour another glass and went to his bed, climbing under the velvet coverings and pulling them over his head. Even with the wine his thoughts were still troubled but his body was heavy with tiredness and as the bed grew warmer he dropped into a deep and dreamless sleep.

Outside the Archon's chamber Edren and Athen kept watch, proud of their duty as the Archon's honour guard. In the palace beyond more soldiers paced the halls and in the city the guards patrolled the twisting, climbing streets. From its high towers Shattershard kept watch on the desert and from their concealment in the sand dunes the Hajhi war-bands watched the city. Higher up in the eastern mountains Ciren and Charm had no need to set a watch, surrounded by a whole Tetrarchic troop, and way above even the tallest mountains the stars wheeled slowly across the sky as the night crossed the desert.

3

Standing next to Laura in front of the black space of the Door in the wood, Zoë felt strange and dizzy. The wine she had drunk earlier was having an effect and she was light-headed, as if she might faint. Laura was talking in a calm, certain voice, her light green eyes meeting Zoë's directly.

'. . . . You understand, don't you?' she was saying. 'You have to keep it secret. But you can come with us, if you like. Would you like to? To see what's on the other side?'

Zoë stared at Laura and she felt something rush up within her, a feeling so intense that she was numb with it and wasn't sure if she was exhilarated or frightened. The words were tumbling from her mouth almost before she knew what she was saying.

'Yes. Yes, please. I'd love to.' Then she immediately felt silly, knowing she was saying the wrong things and wanting to be as cool and relaxed as Laura. 'What's it like, the other side?'

'It's wonderful,' Laura said seriously and then smiled, her eyes shining secretively. 'It's another world.'

'Like Narnia,' Zoë said and then jumped as a voice said behind her, 'Just like that.'

It was Alex, Laura's brother. He was standing only a few feet away from them at the edge of the small clearing and looking straight at Laura. He didn't even glance at Zoë as he asked, 'What are you doing?'

'It's OK,' Laura told him. 'Zoë understands,' she said confidently.

'It's a secret,' Alex said, looking at Zoë. He was wearing his long loose coat and carrying a heavy-looking bag. 'You mustn't tell anyone.'

'I promise,' Zoë said quickly and when he didn't say anything added, 'I won't tell.'

'All right then.' Alex nodded. 'You can come with us.' He turned towards the Door and Zoë hesitated.

'Now?' she asked. 'But . . . but what about the party?' She looked over her shoulder in the vague direction of the house. She could hear still the dull boom of the music in the distance.

'Oh, you don't have to stay long,' Laura said and her voice was so normal that Zoë felt instantly more normal herself. 'But you must see it.'

'Do we just go through then?' Zoë asked and Laura nodded. Stepping back from the archway of greenery she held out her hand in an inviting gesture and smiled.

For another moment Zoë held back and then Alex said in a lordly way, 'There's nothing to be scared of. Look, I'll go first.'

Then he stepped past her and into the black hole of the Door.

Zoë saw him vanish into it as if through a curtain, the blackness swallowing him, and glanced quickly at Laura. She was still waiting patiently and Zoë felt embarrassed.

Before she could start to blush she walked quickly forward and into the darkness. Her face twitched, instinctively expecting to be met with a solid wall. Instead there was only space and a brief flash of darkness as quick as a blink and then she was somewhere else.

It was a golden dazzling somewhere and her eyes squinted up against a sudden wave of light and air. Through her lashes she made out an Alex-shaped blur just a few steps ahead and she forced her eyes open, blinking rapidly to adjust to the abrupt change of scene. Before her it seemed as if a whole world was laid out: a clear blue sky stretched in almost all directions to a limitless horizon. Beneath it, as neat as a child's drawing, was a long, flat, empty expanse of yellow-gold sand. She was standing on a small ridge of brownish rock looking across an immense desert.

Instinctively she raised a hand to shield her eyes. The sun glaring from desert sand could blind you if you weren't careful and, ahead of her, she saw Alex doing the same thing as he fumbled a pair of sunglasses out of one of the pockets of his coat. They were round John Lennon glasses and Zoë giggled in spite of herself. Then she felt someone touch her arm and turned a bit to see Laura, standing next to her. Laura's green dress seemed less exotic against the pale gold sand than Alex's dark brown trench-coat and sunglasses and Zoë looked down at her own outfit automatically, feeling suddenly that her purple striped top was too garish out in this arid expanse of nothing. Then Laura pulled at her arm and gently turned her around and Zoë gasped as she realized that the desert was anything but empty.

The small scattering of rocks they were standing on were just the beginning of a mountain range. From about half a mile away it straggled across the other side of the horizon before rearing up a short distance ahead into a colossal black mountain. No, not a mountain. Zoë's eyes widened as she took in the reality of the thing. What she had at first taken for irregular patterns of the rock were towers and battlements. The mountain was a city.

'You see?' Laura was grinning at her and Zoë saw for the first time that the other girl had freckles, almost invisible against her light skin but brought out by the dazzling sunlight. 'Come on,' Laura said urgently, taking her hand, and ahead of them Alex was already setting off along the ridge of rock towards the mountain city.

Zoë took a step forward and then looked over her shoulder. Behind her was a craggy slab of rock face, an overhang casting a section of it into shadow. But there, unmistakably, was the intense inky black of the Door.

'Yes,' Laura said, pausing briefly and looking with her. 'You can see it on this side too. But we're the only ones who know about it. Now come on.' And she firmly pulled Zoë into a brisk walk.

It didn't take long for the heat to make itself felt. It was past midday in the desert and coming out of an English late autumn the sun was blisteringly hot. Zoë had to stop on the way to the city and ask Laura to wait as she took off the leggings she was wearing under her skirt and stuffed them into her bag. Ahead of them Alex walked on down the side of the rock ridge to join a dusty roadway marked with two lines of irregular stones. It led upwards to the city past a scattering of low sand-coloured buildings and a few odd-looking white tents.

They weren't alone on the road. As it toiled upwards Zoë saw other figures scattered along its length until it came to a massive archway about a quarter up the height of the mountain. The mountain seemed oddly curved towards the peak but Zoë couldn't quite take it in as she walked with Laura up the road. Instead she found herself concentrating on trivial things, like the fact that there was a sort of donkey tied to a post near one of the tents. It had a thick yellowish coat and looked hot and grumpy in the baking sun. Further along a small boy sat by the side of the road behind a little woven mat spread with necklaces made of wooden beads.

As Laura and Zoë passed him he looked up and flashed them a wide white smile, calling out to them.

'*Baku tabina! Akla baka!*'

Zoë frowned, she hadn't thought about the language problem. If this was another world obviously they wouldn't speak English. Then, to her surprise, she saw Laura shake her head and say apologetically, 'Sorry, not today.'

The little boy didn't look surprised or confused but a wheedling tone entered his voice as he lifted a string of beads up invitingly and said again, '*Baku tabina?*'

'No, I'm sorry,' Laura told him firmly and drew Zoë after her along the road.

'He understood you,' Zoë whispered, unable to stop herself glancing back at the small boy and his wares. 'And you could understand him. How come?'

'Magic,' Laura said simply and then laughed at Zoë's expression. 'I'll explain later. Relax, Zoë!'

Zoë shook her head. 'How can I relax?' she asked. 'This is too incredible.'

'I know how you feel,' Laura agreed seriously. 'It's like a fairy tale, isn't it?' Then she smiled secretively. 'But it's real.'

The glaring desert sun beat down on them and Zoë could practically feel it tanning her face and arms. The ground was smooth and solid underfoot, the stone pathway covered with a scattering of small rocks amongst the gritty sand. Ahead of them loomed the mountain with its crenellations and outcroppings of towers and the massive gateway not far ahead.

'It's real,' Zoë whispered to herself under her breath. 'But how?'

Laura, falling into step with Alex only a few paces ahead, didn't hear her and Zoë looked at her new friend wonderingly. It still seemed completely incredible that half an hour ago she had been at a party in Weybridge and now she was walking along a desert road in a strange and unfamiliar world while Laura talked about magic.

'Look, Zoë,' Laura said, turning back to smile at her. 'This is it.'

The gateway loomed above them and Zoë took a few steps to catch up with the others as they stood at the foot of a great archway of rock guarding the entrance into the mountain.

Zoë caught her breath at what lay ahead. The centre of the mountain was an immense bowl-shaped crater, scooped out of the heart of the rock. Up and down the sides of the bowl were steep streets of gleaming black buildings and towers, and stairs climbed up and up the steep sides to join the ring of fortifications at the top of the crater. From the gateway Zoë could see the whole city spread out before her in a dizzying succession of terraces and buttresses up and up to the pale blue desert sky.

'Welcome to Shattershard,' Laura said softly.

Zoë stared around her, trying and failing to take it all in. The streets and terraces were bustling with people dressed in a bewildering variety of styles; from concealing sand-coloured robes to bright silks heavy with jewellery and embroidered lace. In the shadow of the archway a group of men in grey uniforms stood on guard, armed with shining swords and burnished shields. Ahead of them the road was thronged with market stalls and buyers and sellers bargaining furiously under sun-bleached awnings. Coming from the stillness of the desert Zoë couldn't take it in and hardly noticed when Alex took her arm and moved her gently onwards down the road. An armed guard briefly blocked their path but before she could stop Laura had spoken to him and they were waved onwards into the crush of the market.

Alex and Laura walked on either side of her as Zoë dawdled through the stalls. Although the market was uncomfortably crowded, it was getting easier to accept the reality of this world. Zoë had been in many markets just like this in Greece and Turkey and Saudi Arabia. The same tantalizing smells of food and the dazzling colours of heaped fabrics and piles of costume jewellery. People bartered and haggled with each other across the stalls and although Zoë didn't understand the language she recognized the tones of voice: wheedling or disparaging or finally accepting.

The stalls lined the streets in a higgledy-piggledy way and it was a while before Zoë realized that they were moving higher up the inside of the mountain.

'Where are we going?' she asked, turning to Laura on her left hand side.

'To our residence,' Laura said and Zoë nodded, then swung her head back in an amazed double-take.

'Your *what*?' she said incredulously and Laura smiled at her reaction.

'Alex and I have been coming here for some time,' she explained. 'We have a house here.' She gestured up the steep street. 'It's not far.'

Zoë felt mind-boggled and fell silent as they walked onwards. It was honestly more like climbing than walking and the street was beginning to resemble a staircase, leaving her out of breath when they eventually came to a stop.

'We're here,' Laura said, stopping by a long white wall overgrown with trailing purple rock plants. In the middle of the wall was an arched metal gate, ornamented with a design of leaves and flowers. Alex held it open for them with exaggerated politeness and Zoë stepped through it into a courtyard cut into the side of the mountain.

There was a small pond at the side of the courtyard, and Zoë could see a complicated system of gutters draining down into it, presumably to catch rain. On three sides of the square the black rock walls had been smoothed flat and windows and doors were cut into them. The house was about five times as large as Laura's house on Bicken Hill and way bigger than Zoë's house on the army base. Zoë turned around in a circle, trying to take it all in, and feeling distinctly unnerved. What Laura had called a 'residence' was more like a mansion.

'Welcome to our home,' Alex said, leading the way towards a large double door, and Laura smiled at Zoë.

'You're going to love it,' Laura said and led Zoë inside. As they stepped through the doorway Zoë caught her breath and then turned to stare at Laura.

'It's incredible!' she said.

Inside was a large light hall. All the walls were smoothly plastered in white and then hung with pieces of bright fabric. Alex opened the wooden shutters of the windows and immediately pulled across patterned muslin curtains to screen out some of the dazzling sunshine. A stone staircase with carved banisters led up from the back of the room and divided into three when it reached the second storey. When Zoë caught Laura's eyes she just laughed and took her hand.

'Come on,' she said. 'I'll show you around.'

The mansion seemed to go on forever. Arched doorways connected room after room full of carved wooden furniture and glossy chests of drawers, carpets and tapestries and cushions. On the ground floor Laura showed her a more basic-looking kitchen with a pump for water and a less basic bathroom with a hot tub and a cold tub, and a jungle of ferny green plants. Closed panelled doors led to a toilet over a long dark shaft leading downwards and a shower cubicle with a water tank connected by piping to somewhere above. Eventually Laura took her back into the sunshine-filled hall as Alex disappeared somewhere upstairs.

'I still can't quite believe it,' Zoë said, sitting down on one of the cushions as Laura got them glasses of a sort of fruit cordial from the kitchen. 'How can you afford all this?'

'We have friends here,' Laura said with a shrug. 'Officially we're merchants. We started out by bringing things from Earth. Just little things really but we trade all over now. In the city and with the desert people.'

'Amazing,' Zoë said, trying to imagine it. 'How long have you been coming here?'

'About two years,' Laura said, grinning when Zoë's eyes went wide. 'We've got to know Shattershard fairly well.'

'Shattershard?' Zoë tried to remember when Laura had said that name before.

'The city,' Laura explained. 'This whole mountain is the city of Shattershard. It's supposedly run by an Archon, a kind of local king, but really it's part of an empire called the Tetrarchate.' She grimaced. 'The Tetrarchate want to take over the whole of this world but they haven't been very lucky in Shattershard recently.' Laura smiled at that and Zoë wondered what she meant.

'I have so many questions,' she said. 'I don't even know where to begin.'

'Choose one,' Laura said. 'We have plenty of time.'

But Zoë had barely begun to speak when there was a sound outside the door.

Zoë jumped at the noise which sounded sharp like a gunshot. Then she blushed, embarrassed, as the sound came again and she identified it as a hand clap and Laura got up from her own cushion. Craning her head to see the doorway Zoë watched with interest as Laura opened the wooden doors to reveal a girl standing there.

'Jhezra, come in,' she said and the girl entered the room with a few words in a language Zoë didn't recognize. The stranger was dressed in long sand-coloured robes and as she came in she threw back the hood of her tunic to reveal an Arabic-looking face dominated by dark brown eyes and a head of glossy black hair tied back into a long plait. From her waist hung a short curved dagger and a longer curved sword. She stiffened when she saw Zoë and turned to Laura with a few quick words which sounded interrogative.

'This is Zoë,' Laura explained. 'She hasn't been spelled for translation yet though so she can't understand you. She's a friend.'

The girl relaxed obviously and turned to Zoë with a quick apologetic smile and bowed silently pressing her hands together in a gesture that reminded Zoë of Hindus saying 'namaste'.

'Hello,' she said, standing up and trying to copy the gesture the girl had used.

'Zoë, this is Jhezra. One of our friends here.' Laura looked pleased with Zoë's response and the newcomer was smiling as she sat down on one of the cushions. She asked something else in that liquid foreign language and Laura nodded.

'He's here,' she said and went up the stairs where Zoë could hear her calling: 'Alex! Jhezra's here.'

Zoë smiled to herself when Alex came quickly downstairs and Jhezra jumped up again with a brilliant smile. Although Zoë might not know much about Shattershard or even be able to speak the language she could guess what that look meant.

'I'm sorry I couldn't come yesterday,' Alex was saying and Jhezra said something in a tone of voice which Zoë interpreted as meaning 'it doesn't matter', when actually it had mattered but Jhezra was reluctant to admit it. There was a brief bit of conversation which was weirdly like listening to one half of a telephone call and then Alex turned to Laura with a diffident look.

'Jhezra and I have some things to talk about,' he began. 'I'm going to go into the desert for a while.'

'That's OK,' Laura said. 'I'll stay here and show Zoë around the city. I should get her a translation amulet if she's going to get around here at all.' She glanced at Zoë. 'Do you want to come out for a while and buy one? It's much more efficient than a GCSE language course.'

'It sounds great,' Zoë agreed immediately.

Jhezra nodded at her and said something in a polite tone.

'She says she's pleased to have met you,' Alex explained, 'and that she hopes you enjoy your visit to the city.'

Wondering if Jhezra guessed how much of a stranger she was here, Zoë tried a smile on the dark-haired girl.

'Thank you,' she said. 'I think the city's beautiful.'

The girl nodded comprehendingly and her eyes were serious as she looked back at Alex and said something in a low voice.

'Jhezra says thank you,' Alex said carefully. 'But that beautiful to her means the desert in springtime.'

Zoë blinked, surprised, but remembering her time in Saudi she made a guess at the right reply.

'Flowers in the desert are like water for the soul,' she said, paraphrasing something she had once heard her father say.

Jhezra looked delighted and bowed again deeper than she had when they first met. Zoë bowed back and said a polite goodbye as Alex and Jhezra left.

*　　*　　*

Zoë thought that if anyone had told her that she'd be sitting in a mansion with Laura Harrell in a fantasy city in another world she'd have laughed herself sick. But Laura seemed completely at home in the exotic setting and her attitude made Zoë feel more relaxed. When she said something about this to Laura the other girl looked serious.

'This is my real life now, Zoë.' Laura curled up comfortably on the luxurious drift of cushions. 'School just doesn't seem important in comparison.'

'Yeah, I can guess it wouldn't,' Zoë agreed. 'Not compared to this.' She hesitated. 'This world seems kind of dangerous though.' She remembered Jhezra's scimitar and the swords of the gate guards.

'It can be,' Laura said slowly. Then she gave Zoë a sparkling look. 'But don't worry, Zoë, I'll look after you.' She jumped up to her feet, the long green dress swishing as she pulled Zoë up after her. 'Come on, I'll show you the city.'

Outside the mansion the heat hit Zoë like a wave and she blinked in the bright sunlight. Laura noticed and said, 'We should get our shopping done quickly before it gets really hot.'

'What about Alex and his girlfriend?' Zoë asked and Laura gave her a sidelong glance.

'You guessed that?' she said. 'I should tell Alex to be more discreet.' She shrugged. 'They'll be all right. They're used to the desert.'

Laura led Zoë along a twisting path through the streets, explaining the turns as they took them.

'It's important not to get lost here,' she said. 'Especially when you don't know the city. If you do get lost, though, just remember that the residence is on Fiveside by Treetower.'

'I don't see how I can ask for directions if I don't understand the language,' Zoë pointed out and Laura shot her a quick grin.

'That's what we're going to sort out now,' she said and pointed to a building a little way ahead of them.

If Zoë had imagined a magician's shop it would have been dark and sinister, full of skulls and ravens and weird roots and strange things in jars. The shop that Laura took her to was nothing like that. They walked in through the open door into something like a cross between a delicatessen and a jewellery shop. Brightly coloured packages with handwritten labels stood on shelves all around the shop and necklaces hung on a high metal rail behind a long wooden counter. Behind the counter was a heavily pregnant young girl in a green dress a lot like Laura's and she looked up with a smile as the two of them came in.

Again Zoë had the bizarre sensation of listening to half a telephone conversation as Laura talked to the shopkeeper. She didn't look in much of a hurry, listening to some long monologue which seemed to be about the new baby and asking about something she'd ordered a couple of weeks ago, but eventually she gestured at Zoë and said, 'My friend here needs an amulet for translation.' The girl asked a question and Laura paused for thought for a while before answering, 'Oh, writing as well, I suppose. Is there a discount for the two together?'

After a few more minutes of talk the shopkeeper took a long pole with a hook at the end and lifted down one of the necklaces with it. It was a red striped stone with a hole bored through it, hung on a leather cord. As Laura paid for it Zoë tied the cord around her neck and squinted down at the stone doubtfully.

The shopkeeper gave Laura her change and glanced at Zoë with a smile as she looked at the necklace.

'Is it working?' she asked Laura and the girl behind the counter laughed.

'Come again next time,' she said and Zoë's eyes went wide with surprise.

'Th . . . thank you,' she stammered as Laura took her hand and led her out of the shop. 'That's it?' she said as they got outside.

'Impressive, isn't it?' Laura replied.

'Amazing,' Zoë replied, beginning to sound a bit like a broken record but unable to think of anything else to say. 'So whenever anyone speaks it'll sound like English to me?'

'Sort of,' Laura shrugged. 'All translation really means is that you'll understand the sense of the words other people speak. If the only language you know is English then it sounds like English but if you know more than one language the things people say can be translated into whatever word seems the most appropriate.'

'I think I understand,' Zoë said and Laura smiled at her.

'It doesn't really matter,' she said. 'But at least now you can understand what's going on here.'

'Thank you,' Zoë said enthusiastically. 'I hope it didn't cost too much; I should pay you back.'

'Don't worry about it,' Laura told her. 'Come on, let's do some more shopping.'

They wandered together through the city, looking at all the shops and stalls. Zoë was fascinated by the snatches of conversation she heard from the passers-by now that she could understand the language. Laura was happy to point out the different sorts of people they noticed: desert nomads in sand-coloured robes like Jhezra's; merchants dressed in green; city guards in light grey uniforms; and columns of chanting priests in red vestments. Everything and everyone was bright and colourful and Zoë was fascinated by it all. But when she noticed someone wearing black she turned to look in surprise.

'Don't stare,' Laura said quietly in her ear, leading her on. 'You don't want the magician to take offence.'

'The magician?' Zoë asked.

'In black,' Laura murmured. 'Only magic users wear black here. Not all of them but the powerful ones do. It's . . . unwise to annoy them. The ones who wear black are kind of touchy.'

'I'll remember that,' Zoë said but she risked one careful glance back at the tall figure of the magician gliding through the crowds in a stately way as people made room for him to pass.

Laura was a generous friend. As she showed Zoë around Shattershard she constantly stopped to buy her things, chatting to the merchants while Zoë looked around. She seemed to have plenty of the local money and Zoë noticed with amusement that many of the clothes were similar to things she'd noticed Laura wearing at school. In one shop Zoë changed out of her stripy sweater into a loose cotton tunic. At a market stall Laura bargained for a necklace of multi-coloured beads and later she bought a silky headscarf; giving them both to Zoë.

'This is so nice of you,' Zoë said gratefully.

'It's fine, really,' Laura said. 'You don't want to get sunstroke.'

The sun was getting hotter but as she got used to it Zoë didn't notice the heat as much as the bright colours after a wet and grey English autumn. More than anything else she noticed the differences between Shattershard and an English city. As they stopped to rest in a sunny plaza Laura pointed out a puppet show setting up in front of a gathering crowd and Zoë gasped in delight. The little wooden puppets didn't have strings and a white-bearded old man was directing their dancing like an orchestral conductor.

'Is that magic?' she whispered and Laura laughed at her excitement.

'Shall we stay and watch the show?' she asked. Touching Zoë's arm she pointed out a man selling cups of coloured ice to the crowd. 'I'll get us one of those, OK?'

'Sure,' Zoë called after her as Laura ran lightly across the plaza, turning back to watch as the puppets curtsied to the audience holding their little wooden arms out stiffly.

Zoë leant against the stone pillar of a storefront, watching the puppeteer, feeling the warmth of the sun even in the shade. When someone came and stood on the other side of the pillar Zoë glanced sideways for long enough to realize that the figure was dressed in pitch black and hastily looked away again, back to the puppets.

'Well, isn't this a surprise,' a familiar voice said suddenly and Zoë whirled round to meet a pair of scornful green eyes, outlined in striking black kohl pencil.

'Morgan Michaels!' she gasped and the girl in black curled her lip.

'Zoë Kaul,' she drawled. 'That *is* your name, isn't it?'

'Ye . . . yes,' Zoë said uncomfortably, glancing around for Laura and feeling embarrassed when she couldn't see her.

'I suppose there's no need to guess who brought you here,' Morgan said and Zoë felt defensive.

'Laura brought me,' she said firmly. 'Not that it's any of your business.'

'Oh, right,' Morgan said with a sarcastic edge to her voice. 'Look, Zoë, I'm going to do you a favour, OK.'

'OK?' Zoë said with puzzlement and Morgan rolled her eyes.

'I don't expect you'll believe me,' she said. 'But you

may as well know. Laura and Alex aren't who they seem to be. Don't trust them.'

'Oh, come on!' Zoë couldn't believe that Morgan was trying to set her against Laura in so obvious a way. 'Why on earth should I believe you?'

'Why on earth?' Morgan looked at her. 'This isn't Earth, Zoë. It's another world. And you should believe me because it's the truth.'

'So what are they supposed to have done that's so bad?' Zoë wondered for a moment if Morgan was going to be able to think of anything, but after a long moment the other girl spoke slowly.

'They're gun-runners,' she said quietly. 'They sell arms to the natives.'

'You've got to be kidding.' Zoë shook her head. 'Where would they even get guns?'

'It doesn't take actual guns,' Morgan said coldly. 'Use your imagination . . . if you have one.' She flicked her long black hair contemptuously, stepping away from the pillar. 'Enjoy the show, Zoë; you're as much of a puppet as those things.' And with that she tossed her head and stalked off.

Zoë glared after her, thinking Morgan might as well have disappeared in a puff of smoke, she'd been about that dramatic. But the encounter had left her rattled and feeling off-balance. Although she didn't want to believe the girl she had remembered something worrying. The boys from the army base had been lending Alex military handbooks about survivalism and guerrilla warfare. As Laura arrived back carrying two cups of flavoured ice, Zoë decided not to mention meeting Morgan just yet.

4

As Alex and Jhezra left Shattershard together the Hajhi girl had been thinking about Zoë.

'Who is your sister's friend, Iskander?' she asked, as they hastened down the steep streets of the mountain city.

'I don't know,' Alex admitted, remembering Zoë's unexpected appearance at the party on Bicken Hill. 'I've only just met her myself.'

'Whoever she is, she knows people of the sand,' Jhezra said thoughtfully. 'Will you bring her to the desert?'

'She's Laura's protégée,' Alex told her.

'As the mage in black was?' Jhezra looked suspicious. 'Your sister's choice in friends is dangerous.'

'Morgan's not a threat,' Alex tried to reassure her. 'She's happy playing with her magical toys. She won't get in our way.'

'I hope so,' Jhezra told him quietly. 'Because we

already have more problems in our way than we can easily overcome.' Her eyes met Alex's seriously and he nodded.

'I know,' he said, looking up at the battlements as they approached the massive city gates.

Alex had been visiting the Hajhim for nearly two years. When he and Laura had first discovered the Door Between Worlds they'd been a fragmented and disillusioned race, trying to scratch out a living on the margins of the Tetrarchate empire. Now, like Alex and Laura themselves, the Hajhim had grown more confident and daring. With his twenty-first century knowledge Alex was the equal of the Hajhi warriors. He saw himself as Lawrence of Arabia or as a boy-general like Alexander the Great who had also been called Iskander. More than anything else he longed to be properly accepted by the Hajhim and to lead them in battle against the Tetrarchate. The aristocrats of Shattershard considered the fortress city impregnable but Alex had thought of half a dozen ways around its antiquated defences and he felt sure the confidence of the citizens in the black rock walls was misplaced.

Passing under the great arch of the gate Alex smiled to himself, imagining the day when the Hajhim would conquer the city. He didn't bother showing his city pass to the guards. In the middle of the day they were kept busy checking the identification and sponsors of people who wanted to enter the city and had no interest in those who were leaving.

As they headed out of the city Alex stole sideways glances at Jhezra. The regular people of Shattershard had viewed her suspiciously, either jostling her in the crowds or giving her a wide berth on the streets, but she walked with complete confidence, one hand resting lightly on the hilt of her scimitar. Alex admired her for her independence and her fierce dedication to her cause.

'What are you thinking, Iskander?' Jhezra asked with a flash of a smile as she caught one of his glances.

'I was wondering,' Alex said, thinking quickly of something less embarrassing to say, 'how the city would change with the Hajhim in charge.'

'It would become a fortress in truth,' Jhezra said. 'The Tetrarchate would not willingly tolerate a hostile city on their border. They hate us enough when all we have is the desert.'

Alex glanced over at her, walking down the dusty road into the sand dunes, and grimaced at her cold expression, knowing that she was thinking of the Hajhi warriors sent to their death by Tetrarchate troops.

'You love the desert,' he reminded her and Jhezra looked up at him.

'Of course,' she said. 'I love it because it's my home. But I'm not blind. The desert is a barren expanse of nothing. Shattershard is an ugly hunk of rock but it's better than the nothing we have right now. But how great would the Hajhim become if we could hold one of your cities of marvels?'

'Great might not be the right word for it,' Alex said, envisaging the Hajhim pouring through the Door Between Worlds and trying to conquer Weybridge town centre.

'I know what you're thinking,' Jhezra flashed a glance at him. 'That we wouldn't understand your cities.' She smiled tightly. 'And you're right. People can't go from a huge nothingness of sand to a world like yours and expect to understand it. But I ask you, what fortune is it that gives the Tetrarchate their empire of green fields and strong towers, your people their world of wonders, and nothing but sand . . . ' She bent quickly to grab a handful of the gritty stuff before letting it trickle through her fingers, blowing back to the ground in the light breeze. 'Nothing but sand to my people?'

Alex stopped walking to put his arms around Jhezra. They stood together on the sandy road, the city behind them and the length of the desert ahead. Although she let him hold her Jhezra didn't respond, looking away from him to the distant horizon.

'I don't know,' Alex said eventually. 'I don't understand it either. It doesn't seem fair.'

'You haven't lived it, Iskander,' Jhezra said quietly, turning in his arms to look up at him, and Alex tightened his hold on her.

'I've tried to,' he said. 'As much as you've let me.' It had taken him a long time to be accepted by the rest of the warriors and even now some of them were still wary of him as a foreign stranger.

'We're not a very trusting people,' Jhezra admitted, pulling back out of his arms and taking a step down the road. 'Come on, let's walk.' Alex fell into step with her and Jhezra gave him a brief smile as their arms brushed.

'You can trust me,' he told her and Jhezra nodded.

'I know,' she said. 'That's not the problem.' She sighed to herself as they turned off the road and set off into the desert, Jhezra taking the lead now from long experience with the route.

Normally, as they walked the Hajhi girl would explain the desert to Alex, teaching him about the terrain and telling him about their recent skirmishes with the caravans. Today they walked together in silence for a while. Jhezra turned her dark eyes towards Alex, considering him as they travelled and Alex waited, recognizing the look she gave before deciding whether or not to trust him with something. Eventually she came to a decision and spoke out loud.

'It's hard to know what to wish for you,' she said. 'If our plans went wrong and the Tetrarchate crushed the Hajhim, would it be better to know you could be safe in your world? Could I selfishly wish you to be here to share our misfortune?'

'I'd want to stay,' Alex told her. But he frowned, thinking about it, and added: 'But it sounds strange to say that when you're so loyal to your people. It makes me wonder if I'm being unfair to mine.'

'Like Lawrence,' Jhezra asked. 'The soldier you told me about, who was more loyal to the Arabs than his own army.'

'Like that,' Alex agreed but he knew that wasn't the real answer.

Ahead of them were the first concealed indications of the war-camp and as Alex and Jhezra came over the last rising dune and into the dip of the camp, warriors greeted them in a friendly way. As Jhezra led the way towards her tent Alex answered the greetings absent-mindedly, finally following Jhezra inside and sitting down on the rug automatically.

'You look troubled,' she said, sitting next to him and touching his arm. 'What's wrong?'

'It's not really like T. E. Lawrence,' Alex said eventually. 'My leaving home, that is. I wish it was, that would seem a lot grander. Lawrence's ideals were high enough that he was prepared to risk his job in the British army.' He looked at Jhezra. 'What would I be giving up? My absentee parents? A university place? A-level history?' He shook his head. 'It's ridiculous when you think about it. The only thing Earth has to offer is that it's *safe*.'

'That would seem a great deal to me,' Jhezra said.

'And it's nothing to me,' Alex replied. 'I'm tired of being safe. Here I have the chance to really do something meaningful.' He paused. 'I know it's hard for you to understand,' he said.

'No.' Jhezra squeezed his arm lightly. 'I do understand,' she said. 'Your wants are different because you've been brought up differently. I can't understand why you'd want to give up your world when it sounds so miraculous but . . . ' she raised her eyes to his hesitantly, 'but I think I'm selfish enough to be pleased about it.'

Alex couldn't help smiling, leaning down towards her. But just as his mouth brushed hers they jerked apart, sitting up as the sound of some commotion in the camp came through the tent walls.

Scrambling through the flap and blinking in the sudden sunshine, they looked around and Jhezra pointed out one of her friends nearby at the edge of a group of arguing warriors. As they walked quickly to join him Alex recognized him as Tzandrian, one of the few Hajhim he really counted as a friend.

'What's happened?' Jhezra asked and Tzandrian grimaced.

'Our scouts have returned from watching the east hills,' he said. 'A troop of blue-uniformed soldiers have come down from the mountain pass. Five hundred of them or more and they are heading towards the stone city.'

'Tetrarchate troops?' Alex said, hardly able to believe it.

'The Archon must have sent for them to defend the city.' Jhezra clenched her fists angrily. 'It won't help them.'

'No,' Alex agreed quickly. 'We might need to change a few details of our plans but there's no way they can stand up to what we intend.'

Listening to them, Tzandrian laughed suddenly and clapped Alex's shoulder affectionately.

'Thank the gods of fate you came to us, Iskander,' he said. 'You're right. The Tetrarchate won't know what hit them.'

Zoë and Laura got back to the mansion soon after the sun

had passed its zenith in the sky. As they went in through the arched iron gate Zoë noticed an immediate difference about the residence. In the courtyard a little boy with the same black hair as Jhezra was industriously sweeping the flagstones with a long broom. From the first floor a girl with her head wrapped in a brightly coloured scarf was beating a carpet out of the window and the double doors of the mansion stood open to reveal a wizened old man dozing in a rocking chair in the shade of the entrance.

'What . . . ' Zoë turned to Laura with an incredulous look and the other girl laughed.

'Ah,' she said, with a mock-haughty expression. 'I see the servants have arrived.'

'This I really don't believe,' Zoë whispered to her as they went inside.

The old man in the doorway opened a sleepy eye and nodded to Laura as they passed.

'A fine afternoon, Lady Laura,' he said, smiling in a crinkly way at them.

'Hullo, Vesim,' Laura said casually. 'This is my friend Zoë; you'll know her again.'

'Hi,' Zoë said uncertainly and the old man opened his other eye and looked at her for a moment.

'Greetings, Lady Jhzoee,' he said, giving Zoë's name the same jay-zed sound as Jhezra's. 'I'll remember you.' His eyes closed again and Laura grinned, heading on past him and into the house. Zoë followed, glancing back at the dozing figure one last time as she followed Laura up the staircase.

At the top of the stairs Laura led her left down a corridor and into another extravagant room. But before they could sit down a light handclap sounded outside the door and the girl in the headscarf came in without waiting for an answer. She looked about eleven or twelve years old and her big brown eyes were shiny with curiosity.

'Lady Laura,' she said. 'We saw you'd been here already when we arrived. Mother said she hoped you didn't need us for anything?'

'No, it's all right, Ezeki,' Laura said reassuringly. 'We arrived earlier than we expected to. I've been showing Zoë around the city.' She introduced Zoë again and to Zoë's surprise Ezeki made her a fluttering curtsy, spoiling the effect when she burst into giggles.

'Shall I get you something?' Ezeki asked and Laura smiled at her.

'Why not?' she said. 'Can you find us something nice to drink, Ez? And get something for yourself as well.' While the young servant ran off Laura turned to Zoë and explained:

'They're not really servants but Jhezra's people aren't allowed to be in the city unless they're employed by a Tetrarchate citizen and . . . ' she gestured to her long light-brown hair, 'I look enough like the Shattershard people to pass for one.'

'I'm not sure I understand,' Zoë said and Laura shrugged.

'It's not important,' she said. 'Just an exchange of favours really. They get a city pass and I get to pretend I'm a wealthy merchant with servants. It works out.'

Zoë didn't really understand the local politics enough to know if what Laura was saying made sense but the way she put it made it sound like a tax fiddle, something people did to smooth their way through the rules, and she let it pass.

Later that afternoon Laura told her about the similarities between Earth and the Tetrarchate world.

'They run on the same time,' she said. 'That's not like the Narnia world, the same amount of time passes here as there.' She glanced at her watch. 'We've been here four hours so four hours have passed back on Earth and it's gone midnight there.'

'We should get back before your party ends,' Zoë said immediately. 'Or I'll lose my ride back to the base.'

Laura looked at her for a moment and then said slowly, 'Or we could stay a while longer. Alex and my parents are away and with such a big party going on no one'll miss us until late next morning.' She paused. 'If you want to go home, that's fine,' she said. 'I'll just walk you back to the Door. But if you wanted to you could stay and see some more of the city. Your ride will just think you drank too much and crashed somewhere and Alex can drive you back tomorrow.'

'Um . . . ' Zoë tried to think and wasn't sure what she wanted to do. 'Can I think about it for a moment?' she said.

'Sure,' Laura said easily. 'No pressure. But you should stay if you can. You should at least see the palace.'

'Yeah, that would be cool,' Zoë agreed. 'And my dad isn't coming home until Sunday night. I'd be back by then, right?'

'Oh, ages before,' Laura told her and Zoë grinned.

'OK then,' she said. 'Thanks. I'd love to stay!'

Alex still wasn't back when Laura and Zoë got ready to go to court. Zoë couldn't help but smile to herself when she remembered how she had imagined being friends with Laura: hanging out together and swapping clothes with each other. In the Shattershard mansion Laura had wardrobes full of embroidered dresses made of silk and lace as well as tunics and trousers and waistcoats and scarves and cloaks. Little Ezeki helped them get ready, looking Zoë over critically while Laura selected possible outfits.

'I like your hair,' she said shyly winding a tendril of Zoë's curls through her fingers. 'I've never seen red hair before.' She looked at Laura and said, 'Perhaps a red dress, Lady Laura.'

'That might be too much,' Laura said. 'Besides, red is the colour of priests. It might make her look a bit serious.'

'Only priests wear red?' Zoë asked and Laura shrugged.

'Not just them. Nobles really wear whatever they want anyway. But priests' robes are red.'

'But only magicians wear black?' Zoë checked and when Laura nodded she fell silent thinking about the black outfit Morgan had been wearing in the market plaza.

'How about green?' Laura asked. 'Green sort of means merchants and it's reasonably unpretentious.' She smiled. 'Besides I think you'd look good in green.' She spread out a long-skirted dress in a deep forest green with a sparkling trail of grey and silver embroidered leaves and birds scattered across it in swirls.

'It's gorgeous,' Zoë said and was unprotesting when Laura and Ezeki helped her put it on and laced up the back in a complicated design of crossing and over-crossing silver ribbons. While Ezeki sat Zoë down at a dressing table and fixed her hair, securing it high up with silver combs, Laura changed into a blue brocaded tunic top and a skirt made of layers of blue and silver lace. Ezeki wrinkled her nose at it and told Zoë:

'Tetrarchate.'

'She's right.' Laura's eyes met Zoë's in the looking glass and she smiled. 'Blue and silver are the colours of Tetrarchate troop uniforms. But it's not as if anyone's about to mistake me for a soldier in this outfit.'

'What other colours mean something?' Zoë asked, fascinated, and Ezeki paused in her adjustment of the last tendrils of Zoë's hair to say, 'Hajhim wear the colour of sand.' She smiled brightly. 'For ambushes.'

'The Tetrarch and the higher nobles, like the Shattershard Archon, wear white and gold on state occasions,' Laura broke in, frowning at Ezeki. 'And the city police and gate guards wear grey; you saw them when we came into Shattershard.'

Turning away from the mirror Zoë watched as Ezeki helped Laura braid sections of her hair into plaits and clip them together. She used what Zoë recognized with surprise as lots of little blue plastic hair clips in the shape of dragonflies that Laura could have got at the Weybridge shopping centre. Laura saw her looking and laughed.

'I know what you're thinking,' she said. 'It's silly, isn't it, but we honestly do trade in this kind of thing. They're worth about ten times as much here and everyone thinks Alex and I are incredibly cunning merchants to be able to get hold of them.'

'That's crazy,' Zoë said and Ezeki looked puzzled.

'I like the little insect clips. The city ladies won't have seen them yet, they'll be jealous.' She looked approvingly at Laura's hairstyle and Laura smiled.

'They're fine, Ezeki.' She glanced at Zoë. 'And Zoë, you look amazing. Ezeki, you've wrought wonders!'

Ezeki giggled and Laura took Zoë's arm, showing her to a long mirror at the side of the room. While Zoë took in the sight of herself in the green dress Laura asked Ezeki to tell Vesim to call them a carriage. Then she came back to Zoë.

'Excited?' she asked and Zoë took a deep breath.

'Yeah,' she said. 'Nervous too. I don't know what to expect.'

'You'll be fine,' Laura reassured her. 'People are really out of things here. If anyone asks you about where you come from tell them you're from a distant city of the Tetrarchate. But they won't, you know, people are a lot like back home. They'll ask you about music or clothes or if you've heard the gossip.' She smiled. 'Besides I'll be right there. If you feel confused about anything just whisper to me.'

As afternoon drew towards evening lights were lit up and down the twisting streets of Shattershard. Little mountain ponies drew carriages up the wider thoroughfares towards the towers of the Archon's palace. There lights shone from the hundreds of tiny windows as carriage after carriage pulled up to the entranceway and deposited its cargo of nobles. Even in these dark days the aristocracy and the richer guild members of Shattershard still came regularly to court, perhaps even more often now the court gossip spread the latest political rumours. Tonight the palace was crowded even at the beginning of the evening. Rumours were rife that Tetrarchic soldiers had been sighted from the towers and the court was in an excitable mood.

When Laura and Zoë got out of their carriage and stepped on to the shallow curve of steps leading through the palace gates Zoë couldn't help staring all around her, trying to see everything. The court in their glittering clothes and the servants and guards attending them reminded her of fairy tales and fantasy stories. But as Laura led her through the entrance and along a series of galleried rooms separated by still more little staircases, she remembered a trip to France she had gone on at one of her earlier schools. More than anything else the Shattershard palace reminded her of the French royal palace of Versailles with its bright lights and its series of beautiful rooms leading into each other. Compared to the luxury of the palace even Laura and Alex's residence paled into insignificance.

'It's too much,' she said to Laura when the other girl asked her what she thought. 'I mean, it's beautiful but . . .'

She shook her head. 'Confusing. Everything's so gorgeous I don't know what to look at.'

'I felt like that at first,' Laura reassured her. 'But you do get used to it. Just remember that a lot of these people feel intimidated too.'

It was hard to believe. Trying not to look too obvious about it, Zoë stuck close to Laura's side as her friend found them glasses of a strange indigo-black drink that smelt alcoholic like wine, and then continued to trail after Laura as she moved slowly through the crowd speaking to people when she recognized them. Every now and again Laura would whisper something under her breath about one or another of the people they passed, along the lines of:

'That's Jocassin, he used to be big in the guild of merchants here but he lost money a year ago after a lot of his trade caravans fell to bandits. He's pretty bitter about it.' Or: 'The woman in purple over there was the old Archon's mistress. People think she was hoping he'd marry her but he died before he could and now she's after that fellow, he's a lord of some kind, I think.'

'How did the Archon die?' Zoë asked and Laura said quietly, 'An illness. They don't have very good doctors here, not by our standards.'

'Do you trade medicine at all?' Zoë asked thoughtfully and Laura flicked a glance at her.

'Not with the city,' she said. 'Sometimes with the Hajhim.'

As they worked through the crowd Zoë was reminded of the way Laura was at school. Like there, everyone here seemed to know her. Every few moments another person stopped to say hello and bow politely when Laura introduced Zoë as 'a friend visiting the city'. In return Zoë tried to imitate Laura's half-curtsies, noticing that no one here used the *namaste* gesture Jhezra had made nor did any of them have glossy black hair or sand-coloured clothes.

Just as Ezeki had told her she would, Zoë found herself standing out in the crowd. More than a few people openly admired the colour of her hair, telling her how unusual it was in this area and speculating on where she came from. After the first couple of people tried to guess Zoë turned it into a guessing game, agreeing with whatever the third guess was each time. Laura looked approvingly on, while she herself talked to other merchants dressed mostly in green, discussing the status of trade in the city.

When she had finished her glass of dark wine Zoë asked a servant for fruit juice, trying not to get drunk. Laura took more wine and they sat down for a second on an elegant little sofa in a recess of one of the court rooms. But Zoë had barely touched her drink when Laura, looking over her shoulder, said significantly, 'Here comes trouble.'

Looking round, Zoë saw a familiar figure stalking towards them through the crowd, who automatically gave way, apparently by instinct, as they noticed the black clothes she was wearing.

'Look what the cat dragged in,' Morgan said coldly, stopping at their side.

'What do you want, Morgan?' Laura asked, glancing up at her. 'This isn't the place for an argument.'

'Ashamed to be seen with me, Laura?' Morgan asked. 'Now that you've got a new little pet to worship you? All dressed up in your clothes.'

'Hey!' Zoë glared at the girl in black. 'At least I'm not going around pretending to be Darth Vader. Why don't you get over yourself, Morgan?'

For a second Morgan looked surprised. Then she laughed and shook her head. 'You should explain things to her better, Laura,' she said, turning back to the brown-haired girl. 'Otherwise your little pet might get into trouble.'

'I don't think so,' Laura said calmly. 'Zoë's not like you.'

Morgan glared at her and then tossed her head.

'Look, Laura,' she said. 'I'm telling you once, right? Stop mucking about with the Hajhim. Things are dangerous here now and if you don't stop, people are going to get killed.' She turned back to look at Zoë with the same deliberate sneer. 'You should run away home and find some Weybridge townies to worship instead of her highness here.' Leaning forward across the table she said with low-voiced intensity, 'Laura *lies*.'

'Yeah, like I'm going to listen to you,' Zoë said angrily. 'Who asked you to come glooming and dooming around us anyway? What's the matter, Morgan? Isn't this world gothic enough for you?'

Laura laughed out loud and Morgan's face stiffened at the sound.

'You have no idea what you're talking about,' she said, tight-lipped, before looking back at Laura. 'And as for you, I've warned you. OK?' And with that she turned her back and walked off.

Zoë considered calling something after her, still feeling annoyed, but when Laura met her eyes with a grin she subsided.

'God, Laura, what's her problem?' she asked and Laura shook her head.

'She's probably pissed off that I've brought you here. Morgan's been coming here as long as we have unfortunately and she's got a sort of obsession about things staying exactly the same.' She shrugged. 'I'm sorry she was such a bitch to you.'

'That's OK,' Zoë told her. 'I wouldn't listen to anything she said anyway.'

*   *   *

Morgan bit her lip as she walked away from Laura and Zoë, noticing how much angrier she was with Zoë than Laura. When she'd seen the new girl in the Shattershard market place she'd been amazed enough to stop and talk to her and it had been only fair to give her some kind of warning of what she was getting into with the Harrells. But now it seemed as if Zoë was well and truly on Laura's side even though she couldn't possibly have any idea of what that meant.

Stopping around a corner from where she had left the other girls Morgan went to stand at the edge of a balconied area overlooking one of the lower arrival rooms, trying to control her temper. What was Laura doing anyway? she wondered to herself. Why on earth had she brought Zoë through the Door? Morgan clenched her fists. Seeing the two of them tricked out in their silks and laces and Laura with those stupid plastic clips in her hair, pretending that everything was just a silly game, she couldn't believe it. Laura had always been clever back in Weybridge but here in Shattershard she seemed to be always ten steps ahead of anything Morgan imagined she might do.

A gonging sound from below distracted her attention and Morgan glanced over the balcony at the crowd of arrivals below. The gong meant that someone important had arrived and she peered down at the crowd, trying to work out who had merited the announcement. It wasn't hard to tell. Already the courtiers and servants were falling back to allow a group of blue and silver uniformed soldiers to pass. Morgan gasped in surprise. Blue and silver meant Tetrarchic troops and this group must have travelled across the mountains to get here.

Ducking back from the balcony Morgan walked lightly up a nearby set of stairs and around the curve of a sloping stateroom. She'd come to court often enough to know the quickest ways through the public rooms of the palace and this one led to the main Audience Hall. If Tetrarchic troops had arrived in the city they would naturally present themselves to the Archon before anything else and this was where he was most likely to be found.

Coming abruptly into the hall Morgan realized that the news of the Tetrarchic soldiers' arrival couldn't have reached here yet. Aristocrats and priests and some of the richer merchants clustered in groups about the lavishly decorated room and there was a scattering of mages dressed in her own black. At the high end the Archon and his advisers held court from a stepped dais. Almost everyone here was adult and Morgan noticed a few people glancing at her with slight curiosity before looking away again politely. Taking a drink from a passing servant Morgan tried to blend into the edges of the crowd as she skirted the room to where she could get a view of the Archon. She wasn't the only one with the same idea. A few minutes after her arrival more people began to arrive gradually, obviously with the same instinct as her that the soldiers would present themselves formally.

She had guessed right. The Tetrarchic soldiers arrived in the Audience Hall not long after and headed directly for the Archon. By tradition they must have given up most of their weapons at the gate since no one was allowed to approach the Archon with any blade over a certain length. But nonetheless the courtiers stepped hastily out of their way. Tetrarchic troops were alarming enough even without swords. It wasn't hard to guess who their leader was; his uniform was the most decorated and he led the group directly towards the Archon where he paused to make a low bow.

'Greetings from the Tetrarch, Lord Archon,' he said, bending to one knee. 'He sends his best wishes to your city in this time of trouble, and the better to ensure those wishes he sends also myself and my soldiers to your defence. I am General Shirishath and there are five hundred of the Tetrarchate's finest under my command.'

The courtiers held their breath and fixed their eyes on their Archon, wondering how he would respond. Morgan watched Kal intently as well, admiring the calm way his blue-grey eyes studied the general thoughtfully before he spoke.

'We thank you for your courtesy, General, and for conveying the courtesies of the Tetrarch,' Kal said. 'You are welcome to Shattershard.'

As the general straightened from his bow amid the whisperings of the court, Morgan glanced at the soldiers behind him and noticed something odd. Behind the blue-uniformed men and women were two shorter figures. A boy and girl dressed identically in sober black. Both had the same pale blond hair and they watched the Archon and the general with identical pairs of dark purple eyes. As Morgan watched them the girl-twin's gaze shifted across the crowd and met hers. Morgan held her breath as their eyes met and the girl's mouth slid into a slow smile.

5

Kal stared down at Shirishath, his mind racing. As he asked the general if he had made arrangements to house his troops and learned that they were occupying some of the empty barracks near the walls, he tried to work out what he should do. Just the idea of five hundred Tetrarchic troops made it hard to think. The standard city guard of Shattershard could mount perhaps two hundred at the most and the militia another four. Five hundred of the Tetrarch's finest was more than a courtesy, it was an army.

At his side he felt Jagannath lean nearer and he turned to look at the cardinal. Catching his eye Jagannath looked down into the crowd and indicated with a tilt of his head two figures at the back of the group of soldiers. Catching his look General Shirishath gestured and the two separated themselves from the crowd and joined him, bowing to Kal in unison.

'May I present two friends of mine,' Shirishath said,

as they bowed. 'Ciren and Charm. Magicians who have been travelling with our troop.'

'Magicians?' Kal was surprised into saying, and he winced as his response caused the court to mutter and Jagannath to frown. Kal hesitated, staring down into the two identical faces. What kind of general travelled with magicians? he wondered. These two didn't look any older than he was. He noticed that in addition to their magician's black the boy wore an archer's vambraces on his arms and the girl had a pair of wicked-looking daggers hanging at her belt just a hair's-breadth from being long enough to count as swords.

'Lord Archon, I am Ciren, of the Order of the Wheel,' the boy said. 'And this is my twin sister, Charm. The general was kind enough to allow us to travel under the protection of his troop on our journey to see your city.'

'I see,' Kal said. 'Well, you're welcome here, Ciren. Although I admit I have never heard of a magical order called the Wheel.'

'We are simple scholars, your highness,' the girl, Charm, said smoothly. 'We study the different magics used across the kingdoms and city states of the Tetrarchate and beg leave to continue our studies here.'

Kal considered, keeping his face carefully blank. This went a little deep for him to be comfortable. No magician who wore black could be a simple anything and 'continuing their studies' was a euphemistic sort of phrasing. What if their studies involved the kind of destructive magic that could cause havoc in Shattershard? Thinking fast, Kal came to a conclusion of sorts.

'The general has vouched for you and I have said you are welcome here,' he told the twins. 'As long as you obey the laws of our city you may do as you wish in Shattershard.'

'Thank you, Lord Archon,' Ciren said, bowing again,

and the girl at his side expressed her thanks with a sudden smile.

'My thanks also,' she said, softly, still smiling and Kal felt suddenly dizzy, staring down into those huge purple-black eyes. The spiked weight of the heavy Archon's crown pressed uncomfortably tightly on to his head. Gritting his teeth against the sensation Kal tore his eyes away from the girl's and nodded in the way that signified dismissal.

The two magicians melted back into the crowd and Kal invited Shirishath to take a chair on the dais and his soldiers to take part in the festivities of the court almost automatically. When they had distributed themselves he turned at last to Jagannath, looking for approval. To his relief the cardinal seemed calm and Kal lowered his voice to ask, 'Your thoughts, please, Jagannath.'

'As a Tetrarchic general Shirishath's command over his troops is absolute,' Jagannath murmured. 'They take their orders from him alone.' He lowered his voice still further to add, 'They are not subject to city law.'

Kal nodded; the news didn't surprise him. Bending his head nearer to Jagannath he said in a whisper so low that it barely moved his lips, 'The Hajhim won't like this, Jagannath.'

The cardinal's whisper reached his ears faintly.

'Neither do I, my lord.'

Ciren and Charm moved away from the Audience Hall almost immediately after being dismissed. Now they wandered together around the sloping staircases of the public rooms in no particular direction, heads close together as they talked in quiet voices. Charm's lips quirked into a flicker of a smile whenever they passed people of the court but they didn't move to speak to any of the courtiers.

'What do you have?' Ciren had asked as they left the Archon.

'Bide a moment while I think it through,' Charm said. 'What are your impressions.'

'Magic was thick in that room,' Ciren told her. 'More than one magician was there and most of the other courtiers were wearing enchanted items of one kind or another. Translation amulets, protection spells, and a few magical daggers and such. The only item of real power was the Archon's crown, which has some powerful protections set on it. I'd need to spend longer there to tell you what they were.'

'I can make a guess at one of them, at least,' Charm said grimly. 'He was immune to my mind-reading.'

Ciren turned to look at her in surprise. In their travels through the worlds no one had yet proved immune to his twin's unusual talent. As far as he knew his and Charm's magics were unique and they'd never yet met a magician powerful enough to counter them. For the boy Archon to be capable of blocking Charm was an unexpected complication.

'That might be a problem,' he said. 'What do you think?'

'I was able to read his advisers,' Charm said. 'The only one to be reckoned with was the one in red.'

'Red is the colour of priests.'

'He was a cardinal, I think. Named Jagannath. Intelligent and observant, if a little antiquated in some of his views. He's the power behind the throne here.'

Ciren nodded. 'Well, if you can read him then the Archon's crown won't present too much of a problem,' he said. 'But I wonder what other abilities it has.'

'I got something unexpected in there,' Charm said, remembering her arrival in the Audience Hall.

'I saw you smile at someone,' Ciren told her. 'But I wasn't sure who.'

'The girl with green eyes overdrawn with black?' Charm said, prompting his memory. 'Her name is Morgan. Black hair, black garments of an unusual design?'

'Yes, I saw her,' Ciren said. 'Amulets at her belt, silver chain bracelets, and two or three necklaces. Most of the jewellery magical and her own power strong but untrained. Not skilled enough to really deserve the black but that's common enough.'

'Her mind wasn't at all common,' Charm said. 'I only got a flash and she was too complicated to read all at once. But her thoughts were full of alien images. A world I've never heard of and not easy to comprehend. But she's an uninitiated world-traveller, without a doubt.'

'Did she seem hostile to the court?' Ciren asked. 'As if she might be behind this Hajhi uprising?'

Charm shook her head slowly. 'No, she didn't,' she said, thinking. 'If anything the reverse.' She glanced across at Ciren with a glint in her eye. 'She seemed very taken with the Archon.'

'Oh, indeed?' Ciren smiled back at her. 'He certainly looked the part. A young aristocrat to the backbone trying very hard to live up to the role.' He slanted a look at his sister. 'What did you think of him?'

'I hardly know.' Charm shook her head. 'Perhaps I've got too used to seeing people from the inside . . . I only got the vaguest impression. Most of the image I have of him comes from Morgan, the girl in black.'

Ciren met his twin's purple-black eyes and frowned at her. He was used to having Charm inside his mind, comfortable enough with her that he found it no distraction to have her in the back of his head when he used his own power. But for the first time he found himself wondering how it really affected his twin to read other people so easily. When Charm met his thoughtful look with curiosity he quickly dropped the thought, not sure it was one he wanted her to read from him.

'So our next move then?' he asked. 'Return for a further reading on the Archon's crown and his advisers? Find Morgan and question her? Or there is the matter of the Doors.'

'Yes, you sensed more than one . . . ' Charm paused and drummed her fingers absently on the balustrade of the staircase they were descending. 'We should take the one inside the city first. Then we can investigate the desert. I'd like to take some more readings on the situation with these Hajhim before we head out into the sand.'

'Agreed then.' Ciren paused. 'But first I think we had best find some lodgings before it gets too dark.'

'Practical as always, twin,' Charm said lightly. 'Let's enquire for the local magical guild-house then. With any luck it'll give us a chance to track down the mysterious Morgan at the same time.'

As Charm and Ciren left the Archon's court as subtly as they could, disregarding the curious eyes of the courtiers, others were still arriving at the palace. Although Shattershard had its taverns and theatres the palace was the focus of entertainment for the aristocracy even though the Hajhi attacks on the caravans had made it less luxurious of late.

From his seat on the dais Kal looked at the massed hordes of courtiers and wondered what they were really thinking. As the city's Archon he lived in the centre of the political web but it seemed to mean that he was less aware of what the rich and powerful of Shattershard actually thought. All he ever saw was the formality owed to his status, and although he knew that there were intrigues and plots working out all around him he was incapable of watching and assessing them for himself; for that he had to rely on advisers like Jagannath.

Shifting uncomfortably in his seat, Kal saw Jagannath glance at him and abruptly he stood up.

'I think I'll take a walk for a while,' he said, pitching his voice towards the cardinal but glancing back at his honour guards. 'I believe we've completed the scheduled audiences today.'

'Yes, Lord Archon,' Jagannath agreed, standing and bowing with the rest of the advisers as Kal walked down the dais steps. Edren and Athen stepped smoothly into place behind Kal as he spoke briefly to a few of the other advisers. On one of the lower levels, the Tetrarchic general, Shirishath, was discussing the disposition of troops with the captain of the city guard and Kal's eyes flicked over them as he passed. There were so many discussions, so many plans made, and even though he was the one with the power to make decisions, when it came to the point he felt lost in the wash of opinion.

As Edren and Athen followed a discreet distance away, Kal walked thoughtfully along the long sloping galleries of the public area of the palace. Courtiers bowed to him as he passed but he didn't stop and speak to anyone, preferring the higher balconies where he could look down on the crowd and watch individuals unobserved. It worried him that there were so many he didn't recognize. Catching a glimpse of the twin magicians leaving by one of the side entrances of the palace, Kal wondered how many other unknown qualities were concealed by the regulars at his court. Undoubtedly the Hajhim would have their spies and so would the Tetrarchate, and, even apart from them, every single person who came here to gossip and spread the news had their own personal aims and ambitions, each by necessity conflicting with those of someone else.

Pausing by the edge of an overhanging stairway, Kal let his eyes drift across the revellers, recognizing some and wondering about others. That woman in blue with the tinkling laugh who had tried so hard to attract his father seemed to have found a new quarry. That unassuming girl who had been elected to the guild of merchants a few months ago seemed to have acquired a friend with a glamorous cascade of tawny red-brown curls. Trebbern the merchant was trying to entertain her with a valiant attempt at juggling green-fruit. Kal sighed and rested his arms on the balcony, glancing back over his shoulder at Edren and Athen.

The two boys stood to attention behind him, scanning the crowd themselves for anything that could present a threat. At his look, Athen's expression changed from alert to enquiring, obviously wondering if the Archon wanted anything. Kal sighed, remembering when he, Athen, and Edren had been friends, conspiring together to escape their tutors and explore the streets of the city. Athen's parents were aristocrats who had sent their son to perform military service at the Archon's court as a matter of course. Edren's father was a magician who had often advised Kal's father and, since Edren had little talent for magic, had sent his son to study with the court tutors and weapons trainers. Kal had known them both vaguely for the past ten years and as friends for the last two or three. Now, the carefully detached expressions on his bodyguards' faces made him realize how rarely it was that he spoke to them. Since he'd become the Archon they had faded further and further into the background behind him.

Realizing that Athen's enquiring look was shifting into confusion, Kal said out loud, 'I wonder why all these people keep coming here, night after night. You'd think they'd have something better to do with themselves.'

They moved up a little closer to join him at the balustrade.

'Most of these here are merchants, my lord Archon,' Athen said diffidently. 'Everything they do is for profit one way or another.'

'Most people in Shattershard are merchants,' Kal said, repeating the substance of one of his recent meetings with his advisers. 'Everything we have here comes from trade since the desert has little enough to offer.'

'My lord Archon, there are magicians . . . ' Edren said carefully.

'It's true,' Kal agreed, smiling a little to indicate that he wasn't annoyed with the correction even as he winced internally at the distance he could feel between them. 'But the cities of the Tetrarchate have magicians in their thousands. In the capital something like one in every eight people is a practising magic user.' He shrugged awkwardly and added, 'Unfortunately, unless we can eat it or sell it, magic's not much use to us right now.'

Athen and Edren exchanged glances and then Athen stepped a little closer and lowered his voice to say, 'My lord . . . Kal . . . What do you think will happen?'

Kal hesitated. He had asked for this. By trying to talk to his bodyguards as friends he'd opened the way for them to ask a question that he couldn't reply to honestly. His father and Jagannath had taught him that there were some things that he could only respond to as the ruler of the city. He might be worried about the strength of the Hajhim and the dangers of having so many Tetrarchate troops in the city, but he couldn't admit to that if there was any chance it might be repeated.

'I think that Commander Shirishath's troops will teach the Hajhim the foolishness of interfering with Tetrarchate trade.' He paused and then added levelly, 'It's unfortunate that it should have come to this but it seems as if Shattershard's trade problem is about to be ended by the empire.'

'Thank you, my lord,' Athen said politely, stepping away again, and Kal felt a chill in his words as Edren stepped back as well, again returning to their formal stance.

Swallowing a lump in his throat Kal turned back to look over the balustrade again. He knew his bodyguards realized that he hadn't been open with them and he didn't know how to explain why. He wondered how his father had managed to have friends at all.

He stared down into the crowd, trying to keep his face expressionless in case anyone was watching him. Increasingly events seemed to be being taken out of his hands. He didn't doubt that Shirishath's legion would attack the Hajhim but he feared that, far from having their problems solved by the action, Shattershard would be caught right in the middle and he doubted that there was anything he'd be able to do about it.

Abruptly he moved away from the side of the staircase and started down it, hearing Edren and Athen fall into step behind him with a twist of discomfort and deliberately ignoring it. If there was nothing else he could do, he could put on a show of relaxation for the court, hoping that the semblance of calm would quell any fears the people had about so many Tetrarchate troops occupying the city. Stopping a passing servant with a flick of his eyes he lifted a glass of black wine from the tray the man was carrying and took a long sip from it before stepping down into the crowd.

Zoë was feeling tired. They'd spent half a day in Shattershard since leaving Earth and she'd had a whole day at school before that. Until now there had been too much to take in to really think of it but now her body was reminding her that she hadn't slept in twenty-four hours.

Laura was obviously in her element, talking to hordes of acquaintances and introducing Zoë to each of them so that they weren't much more than a blur of names. But just as Zoë was trying unsuccessfully to stifle a series of yawns Laura drew her out of the crowd.

'I think it's time to leave,' she said and Zoë agreed sleepily. 'I'd suggest we slept at the residence,' Laura continued, 'but you should get home and there's been a lot to think about.' She smiled at Zoë. 'Come on, let's call a carriage.'

'Thank you,' Zoë said, as they left the palace. 'It's really been amazing, Laura. I'm just suffering from information overload a bit, I think.'

'Don't worry about it,' Laura assured her. 'Next time I bring you here I'll give you more warning.'

As they found a carriage and Laura gave orders to the driver, Zoë felt reassured by the other girl's assumption that she would be welcome to come back. Now that they were about to leave Zoë was aware of just how much the other world had swallowed her into its fantastic magical atmosphere. Earth and Weybridge and the garrison seemed a million light years away. The bowl of sky above the mountain city had shifted towards the blue-black of night, and Zoë saw Laura glance at her watch briefly, looking at the sky.

'I hope Alex's back,' she said out loud. 'We can't leave it too long to leave the city.'

Zoë felt a clench of nerves at that and sat up straighter, looking out of the carriage window at the twisting streets for any recognizable features. But in the dark the city looked different, the buildings harder to spot in the massive rock walls, and she was surprised when the carriage eventually swerved round a sudden corner and drew up in the residence courtyard.

She got out first and, while Laura paid the driver, looked around. At the doorway the ancient doorkeeper, Vesim, was still sitting, but as she and Laura entered the house Zoë saw a group of people in sandy robes sitting quietly in the hallway and talking amongst themselves. She looked for Jhezra automatically and didn't see her but to her surprise spotted Alex sitting at the edge of the group.

'You're back then,' Laura said, coming to meet him, and Alex scowled at her.

'I've been back for ages,' he said. 'Where were you?'

'At court, obviously,' Laura said coolly, gesturing at their clothes. 'Don't criticize, Alex. I found out something interesting while I was there.'

'Oh?' Alex's expression changed but Laura shook her head.

'I can't tell you now,' she said. 'Zoë and I have to change if we're going to be in time for the gate.'

'Go on then,' Alex said. 'We'll wait for you.'

As Zoë took off the fabulous green dress and changed back into her skirt and jumper she wondered if, for Laura, English clothes were like fancy dress. Laura shrugged quickly out of her own costume, leaving it lying on her bed with the green dress she had come in and changed into a pair of trousers and a floppy-sleeved shirt. Not for the first time that day Zoë wondered how her new friend managed to lead this double life; but she had no time to ask her. As soon as she was ready Laura led her back downstairs and at their appearance the group of people waiting got up. As they left the house together Zoë recognized the little maid Ezeki and smiled at her. She didn't recognize all the others, some of whom collected a donkey from the side of the courtyard, loaded with packs, and led it along behind them as they left the residence.

They made an odd group, Zoë thought, leaving the city. It was getting cold in Shattershard now and the brisk walk through the empty streets was waking her up again. Laura had told her that the Hajhim had to leave every night and she remembered how there had been none of the nomads at the court. Now, as they wound their way down the streets to the main gate, she saw other Hajhi people headed in the same direction. When they came to the gate itself she saw that she and Laura were the only people leaving the city who noticeably didn't have the dark hair of the nomads. Despite his trench-coat Alex more or less blended into the rest of the travellers.

'Stay in the middle of the group,' Laura said quietly beside her. 'The guards won't check passes but it could be awkward if they see us leaving the city so late.'

'OK,' Zoë said nervously. But in the shadows of the entrance the guards were keeping well back from the Hajhim, waving them through without looking at any of them in particular.

Even as they were going through the massive stone gates, a team of men were hauling on an enormous wheel and Zoë heard a sound in the rock walls of the mountain like the gushing of water from high up. A bell rang out loudly in the city behind them and the gates began gradually to close. Turning round to watch Zoë saw them shut with a low boom of sound that echoed thrummingly down the mountain. Beside her Alex had also turned to watch the gate shut and as they set off down the sandy road into the desert he fell into step with her.

'It uses a system of hydraulics,' he told Zoë conversationally. 'Water is caught and trapped at the height of the city and lifted up from springs underneath the mountain. Then it's channelled through a system of wells, fountains, and reservoirs including the gate hydraulics and finally flushes into the sewer. It's practically industrial age technology.' His eyes were distant as he added: 'Just think what they could do with steam power!'

'Have steam trains?' Zoë suggested, trying to keep up with what Alex was talking about. It was weird that despite having the opportunity to visit this magical world he was so interested in hydraulics and the layout of sewers. Zoë wondered if all older brothers were the same; all the ones she'd ever met were obsessed with either sport or science or both. From the way Alex was talking it sounded as if he'd have liked to turn Shattershard into a city just like ones back on Earth.

'Really, though, it would be better to bypass the industrial and atomic age now that we know all about that,' he was saying. 'I've wondered whether you could use magic to initiate nuclear fusion.'

'That sounds dangerous,' Zoë said thoughtfully and Alex looked disparagingly at her.

'No,' he said. 'You're thinking of nuclear *fission*. That's the one that's dangerous.'

Zoë rolled her eyes and wondered if it was also true that all older brothers believed that no one except other boys their own age could possibly know anything at all about science or sport.

'I know the difference between fission and fusion,' she said. 'We had a physics lesson on the atom. I still think that it sounds dangerous.'

But Alex wasn't really listening to her, already talking about the possibilities of solar power and the desert.

Some distance away from the mountain the Hajhi travellers stepped off the road and set off on a kind of track into the dunes. Zoë watched them leave, feeling strange now it was just her and Laura and Alex retracing their footsteps back to the Door they had come through during the day. But this time she tried to pay more attention to the route they took. If anything had happened to Alex and Laura she could have been stranded in Shattershard if she hadn't known the way back, so now she did her best to look around despite the darkness that surrounded her.

By the time they arrived at the low outcrop of rocks where the Door was, night had fallen and stars were coming out high in the sky. Unlike in Weybridge, the sky was unpolluted except for a slight greyness around the mountain city itself and the stars were more like flares than pinpricks, creating whirlpools of light in the vast ceiling of the sky. Zoë tipped her head back, amazed at how many she could see, and then shivered suddenly when she remembered that these could not be the same constellations as on Earth.

'Come on, Zoë,' Laura said softly, touching her arm. 'The Door's over here.' Zoë quickly stepped to her side, feeling for her footing on the uneven rocks. Laura guided her ahead and Zoë stretched her hands out, feeling her way.

She didn't realize that she had found the Door until she was through it. Just as coming into the desert she had been startled by the transition from an English autumn evening to the blazing sunshine of the Tetrarchate world, this time she blinked at the shift from the black desert night to cold watery sunshine and the sudden smell of fallen leaves.

They were back on Earth and back in the Weywode Forest behind the Harrells' house on Bicken Hill. Ahead of Zoë, Alex set off back towards the house, slinging his empty bag easily over his shoulder as he walked. Behind her, Laura emerged from the Door, her figure appearing gradually like a reflection stepping out of a mirror.

'Like Alice through the Looking Glass,' Zoë said out loud and Laura smiled at her.

'Or Alice in Wonderland,' she added stepping away from the Door and in the direction Alex had taken. 'But it's time to get back to the real world, Alice.'

If there is such a place, Zoë thought to herself.

6

When the sonorous tones of the bell that signalled the closing of the gate rang out across Shattershard, Morgan had had to crane her head to hear it over the sounds of the court entertainments. When she'd left the Audience Hall she'd found her way to this square, flat roof-garden set amid the battlements and towers of the palace. Witch-lights in each corner of the square provided a flickering light but the air was cold and breezes whipped round the tower heights.

It was such a dismal place that no one else had stepped out of the function rooms to join her and that suited Morgan well enough. Back in the throne room she'd felt suddenly faint and she'd come out here to get some air. Now, leaning against the cold black stone of the crenellated walls, her head was becoming clearer and an uncomfortable suspicion was growing in her head. The wave of dizziness had coincided with her meeting the eyes of the girl in Shirishath's retinue and she'd stayed long enough to hear the twins identify themselves as mages called Charm and Ciren.

Ever since she'd first discovered Shattershard, Morgan had been fascinated by magic. Originally she'd thought she could find out from the magicians of Shattershard something about the Door Between Worlds. Although Laura and Alex had sworn her to secrecy about its existence, as she'd seen it there was no rule against seeing if the guild of the magicians had books that might explain it. To her frustration she hadn't been able to find out anything about Doors, but in the process she'd learned something even more important. Magical ability wasn't all that rare. Although there were enchanted items and amulets for sale in the markets of the city, the real powers of magic lay in latent mental powers that anyone might have.

As far as Morgan was concerned, that alone would have been enough to make Shattershard a better place to be than Weybridge, even if she hadn't had other reasons to dislike her own world. The discovery that she had the ability to learn magic herself had sealed her decision. Unlike Laura Harrell, Morgan wasn't someone who got noticed, and her black Gothic clothes had only made her more invisible. People like Zoë deliberately avoided her if they wanted to fit in. In Shattershard her black clothes had done exactly the opposite. From the first moment she'd walked into the city people had thought she was a powerful magician and while Laura and Alex had laughed at the assumption Morgan had decided to make it a reality.

Just one of the things that annoyed her so much about the Harrells was that they were so bound up in their political machinations that they had never had much interest in magic and thought of it as all conjuring and illusion. Morgan took her magic seriously and other people's even more so. She knew that wearing black made her appear more powerful than she actually was and half the jewellery she wore was supposed to warn or protect her against magical attacks. Although none of it had given any sign anything was wrong Morgan really doubted that the purple-black stare of the girl-twin could be unconnected to her sudden dizziness.

'It felt as if she was reading my mind,' she whispered to herself and shivered against the cold stone wall.

A noise behind her made her start and whirl round to see the doors open from the court gallery behind her and the shadows flicker as dark figures moved out on to the roof garden.

Kal had wandered aimlessly through the court rooms, drinking a second glass of wine when he finished his first, and talking idly to people who approached him. At all times he tried to sound calm. Even though half these people probably thought of him as a child still, it would only convince them of it if he allowed them to see his true feelings. As he mingled with the courtiers he saw more than a few of the young aristocrats and elite who'd studied or trained with him but he didn't stay to talk long. As with Athen and Edren following formally behind him, Kal didn't know how to cross the distance between himself and the people who'd been his friends.

Handing his second empty glass to a servant, Kal picked up a third from a side table and moved away out of the crowd and through a set of doors leading out to one of the many tower-top balconies of his palace. As he approached the door, Athen automatically stepped forward to open it and pass ahead of him, while Edren fell into step behind. Outside, the cool darkness was an abrupt change from the light and warmth of the court and it took him a moment to realize that he was not alone in the small square.

'Excuse me,' he said, seeing the shape of a figure standing at the edge of the battlement wall. 'I didn't mean to disturb you.'

'That's . . . that's all right . . . Lord Archon,' a girl's voice said awkwardly and from the intonation of the words he recognized that they were being translated to him by the magics in the crown he wore. The girl bowed and stepped back as if she was about to leave and Kal raised a hand.

'No, stay, please.' He glanced back at Athen and Edren, gesturing to them to wait at the door before coming forward to join her at the wall.

'As you wish,' the girl said, dipping her head so that a curtain of jet black hair fell forward to screen her face.

As he reached her side Kal realized with a shock that she was younger than he was and wondered why there were so many young black-robed magicians around. Unlike Ciren and Charm, this girl looked shy, hiding her face half behind her hair so he got only the impression of green eyes streaked with black.

'I don't think we've met,' Kal said gently, thinking she looked frightened. 'May I ask your name?'

Pushing long tresses of her hair back with a nervous hand the girl looked up at him, smiling hesitantly.

'I'm Morgan.' She blushed noticeably as she added, 'I don't know if I should bow or curtsy, your highness.'

'There's no need,' Kal told her, smiling back and feeling amused for the first time that day. 'I can tell by my translation spell that you don't speak our language. Where are you from, Morgan?'

Morgan looked up at him with a sudden thoughtfulness that made him realize she wasn't that young after all. It was the look of someone about to lie.

'From a long way away,' she said, looking down at the stone wall and a few strands of hair escaping to hide her face again for a moment.

'Indeed.' Kal narrowed his eyes, looking at her, and asked suddenly, 'From the same place as Charm and Ciren, by any chance?'

At that Morgan looked up quickly at him, her green eyes wide with obvious confusion, almost ingenuous enough for Kal to think her lying to him again until she spoke.

'No!' she said, shaking her head. 'Really no, honestly. I can see why you might think that but really . . . ' She swallowed her words and shook her head again. 'I don't have anything to do with them.'

'But you knew who they were?' Kal said and Morgan straightened up defensively.

'Only because I heard them introduced in the Audience Hall,' she said definitely. 'They . . . I don't know where they're from . . . but I think they must be powerful magicians.'

'Like you,' Kal said testingly and Morgan shook her head.

'No, your highness. Not like me.' She bit her lips and looked away, a bitter expression crossing her face. 'I'm not . . . ' she hesitated. 'I'm not really much of a mage. Where I come from wearing black means something different.' She looked at him earnestly, obviously hoping that this would help him believe her, before saying hesitantly, 'I think Charm cast a spell on me earlier.'

Despite trying to seem calm, Kal was surprised by that and he knew he showed it. But this girl wasn't reacting like an experienced courtier. If anything she was less sophisticated than the young debutante girls who came to formal balls at the palace. In less than five minutes she'd admitted to not really being entitled to wear the black of a powerful magic user and he had a feeling there was more to her story than just that. But her mention of Charm using magic distracted him enough to ask, 'What kind of spell?'

'I'm not sure,' Morgan shook her head again. 'I have protection against illusion magic and warning amulets for anything dangerous so it can't have been that. But when she looked at me . . . ' She frowned. 'When she looked at me, I felt dizzy.' She met his eyes seriously and her voice shook a little as she said softly, 'I felt as if she was reading my mind.'

'You did?' Kal dropped his own voice instinctively, feeling the chill of the night breeze with a sudden shudder. 'Is that possible?'

'I don't know.' Morgan's voice sounded thin and frightened and she hunched into the stone wall uncomfortably. 'I haven't heard of anyone in this . . . in this city or anywhere else in the world . . . having the power to read minds. Not outside legends and stories. But . . . '

'But what?' Kal realized that he had moved closer to Morgan as she looked up into his face with a sudden blush. But he didn't move back as she stammered an answer.

'But . . . but um . . . there's something I read said there are . . . there are ''more things in heaven and earth than are dreamt of in our philosophy''. And there are things that I know are possible that aren't written down in the books of magic here or in the books of . . . from the place . . . the place I come from.'

Kal looked down at Morgan and decided to believe her for now. Even though he could see her obvious reluctance to tell him where she came from, she seemed genuine to him and her hesitation looked like honest uncertainty rather than an act. Smiling down at the girl he admitted to himself that his willingness to believe her was at least in part because she was so young and pretty and so obviously unsettled by having him so close to her. Her blush came and went rapidly and he wondered how often she'd stood in the shadows in the Audience Hall watching him.

'I won't press you to tell me more about your home,' he said smoothly, moving back from her and sipping from his forgotten glass of wine. 'But I would like to know more about you.' He smiled deliberately and watched her blush again as he saluted her with the glass. 'Can I persuade you to join me for some wine?'

Ciren and Charm had found their way to Shattershard's magical guild-house without any difficulty. In any city with a reasonable number of magic users there would be a place where they met to arrange workings and exchange information. In small towns these places were simple tea houses or meeting rooms and in the larger cities of the Tetrarchate they were huge palaces of learning and politics which reminded the twins of the Great Library of the Collegiate. In Shattershard the guild-house was a large, two-storey building jutting out of the mountainside some distance down and counter-clockwise from the Archon's palace.

The main door opened into a soberly decorated entrance hall where a scribe sat working at a desk, glancing up as the twins came through the door with an expression of carefully disinterested attention. It hadn't taken them long to establish their credentials as visiting mages and to learn about the functions offered by the guild-house. In exchange for paying membership dues, they could use the libraries, the meeting, reading, and experimentation rooms; further dues would allow them to eat in the refectory, and for a lodging fee they could rent sleeping rooms in the building.

They paid in Tetrarchate stamped currency and the clerk entered their details in several different ledgers before inviting them to sign and giving them careful instructions to find the rooms they had rented. Only as they were about to leave him did Charm say casually, 'Oh, one last thing. Could you possibly tell us if a girl called Morgan is registered here?' She accompanied her words with a slight smile and was pleased to sense a recognizable image from the scribe's mind of the girl she was asking after.

'There is a Morgan,' he said. 'The name sounds familiar.'

Charm frowned, certain from the man's mind that it was more than familiar. But Ciren ended the scribe's hesitation by leaning past her to drop another couple of coins on the desk.

'Does that help your memory?' he asked and the scribe smiled pleasantly.

'It's coming back,' he said. 'I believe she rents rooms here herself.' Opening up one of the ledgers he ran his finger down a couple of pages before nodding. 'Yes, room thirteen is occupied by a Morgan.' He paused. 'Will there be anything else?'

'No, thank you,' Ciren said softly and Charm nodded her head at him, joining her twin as they set off up a shadowy flight of stairs into the back of the guild-house.

The rooms when they found them were austere but reasonably comfortable, opening off a long dusty corridor and, as they had requested, connected to each other by an additional door. Leaving their two travel packs by the door, Charm hung up her cloak and took off her sword belt while Ciren explored the rooms.

'No listening spells,' he said, coming back to his twin. 'But overlapping layers of silence enchantments on the walls and floors. Furniture spelled against fire and there are warning alarms for major power-workings although not minor ones.'

'We're probably expected to use the experiment rooms for that,' Charm said. 'I wonder what sort of magics they're used to here?'

'Unlikely to be up to the average level of the Tetrarchate,' Ciren told her. 'This city has certain natural advantages and an impressive aesthetic design but it's a typical borderland outpost in a world where power is centralized.'

Charm nodded as Ciren retrieved their book of notes from his pack and a selection of quill pens.

'I'm wondering if this assignment is likely to turn dangerous,' she said. 'Ever since we reached the desert we've been forced to revise our hypotheses about this place.' She came to sit opposite Ciren at the table, crossing her legs underneath her in the high-backed chair. 'It's clear that someone has been playing power-games with this city. Have you ever seen such a mess?'

'It's all over the map,' Ciren agreed, turning to a fresh page in the book and picking up his pen. 'This agitation from the Hajhim has given the Tetrarchate just the excuse to take over under the guise of "protecting" Shattershard. From the looks of this city, Shirishath's five hundred is definitely overkill.'

'If events turn dangerous we'll have to fight our way out,' Charm reminded him, her glance shifting to her two short swords and the curved bow resting next to Ciren's pack.

'It won't be the first time,' Ciren replied, smiling to reassure her and Charm met his eyes with a glint of amusement.

'True enough,' she said. 'What is it about world-travellers that brings on this king-making fixation?'

*　　*　　*

It was late at night when Kal reluctantly said goodbye to Morgan and called for a servant to find her a carriage home. They'd talked together for hours and, although he still hadn't managed to get her to give up her secrets, he'd found he was really enjoying himself for the first time for what seemed like ages.

Morgan wasn't from Shattershard and, as it gradually became clear, nor was she from anywhere even remotely like Kal's city. He racked his brain to think of a place anywhere radically different enough to explain the girl's curious naïvety on some subjects and her obvious experience with others. He thought he might have some idea when he'd persuaded her to talk about magic. From what she told him about her abilities it sounded as if she was a strong natural mage but the way she talked about magic was with a sort of stunned wonder that gave him pause for thought. Her home might be a place with few magic users, he considered, wondering if she came from some barbarian land beyond the borders of the Tetrarchic empire. But nothing about Morgan was as easy to understand as that and her speech patterns were anything but backward even if her court manners were unpolished.

He continued to puzzle over her identity long after she had left. The rest of the courtiers were departing as well, his advisers had retired for the night, and General Shirishath had left a message requesting a meeting with him the next day. Walking thoughtfully back to his rooms and leaving Athen and Edren at the door, Kal told himself that there was more than one good reason for seeing Morgan again. Not only was there the mystery about her background but her reaction to Ciren and Charm to consider. But he didn't lie to himself about the fact that the main reason he wanted to see her was that she was the first person he'd met since becoming Archon with whom he didn't feel he was just playing a part. That night he slept without needing the wine pitcher placed ready in his rooms and dreamt confusedly of mages with white hair and black hair scattered through the palace like game pieces on a board.

He woke the next morning with a sudden alertness just as the witch-lights in his room were brightening from the low glow they maintained through the night to an imitation of dawn. Feeling actually awake in the morning was a pleasant change from his usual stumblings into consciousness and he dressed quickly, surprising the night guards at the door of his rooms when he came out.

They recovered themselves adroitly and fell into step with him as he headed down the sloping corridors of the palace to the private audience room where he usually met his advisers. Halfway there Athen and Edren found him and changed places with the night guards, looking surprised themselves when Kal tossed them a friendly smile. Determined to do something positive today, he headed into the audience room with a confident walk and came to a halt just past the threshold. Inside, Cardinal Jagannath and General Shirishath were standing and glaring daggers at each other.

'This will be a horrible mistake!' Jagannath was declaiming at the top of his voice and Kal's good mood sank like a stone.

'It is necessary . . . ' Shirishath began before he noticed Kal's arrival and both men turned and bowed low.

'Forgive us, my lord Archon,' Jagannath said, regaining control of himself. 'We did not see you come in.'

Shirishath settled for bowing a second time as Kal stepped between them and took his seat at the head of the room.

It didn't take long for him to discover what they'd been arguing about. Barely had he sat down when they were back into it again, Jagannath almost drowning out

Shirishath when he first tried to speak, a breach of etiquette that made Kal realize quite how alarmed the cardinal was.

'Let the general speak his piece,' he was forced to say and Jagannath subsided into an uneasy silence.

'My thanks, your highness,' Shirishath said. 'I have come here today as a courtesy to inform you of the orders the Tetrarch has given me. As of this morning, it is my intention to place this city under martial law and forbid the entrance or egress of any persons identified as Hajhim.'

Kal stared at him. At the door even Edren and Athen forgot themselves enough to glance at each other for a split second before flicking their eyes back to dead straight ahead.

' . . . regret this necessity,' Shirishath was saying as Kal sat frozen in front of him. 'But the Tetrarch believes that these nomads have become too serious a drain on local resources and the time has come to eradicate the problem. Shattershard may be a city state but in matters of imperial interest you must defer to the wishes of the Tetrarch.'

Kal wet his lips to speak but Jagannath was answering the instant Shirishath paused for breath.

'We don't deny the power of the Tetrarchate,' he said quickly. 'But such a move will inflame the Hajhim. They will never lie down for such treatment. To deny them access to the city is tantamount to a declaration of war.'

'Then war it will be,' Shirishath said coolly. 'My five hundred can easily overcome these desert riff-raff.' He paused to direct his next words at Kal. 'With or without your assistance, Lord Archon.'

While Kal was seeing his good mood rapidly deflate, Morgan was suffering her own shock. She'd got back to the magic guild-house late, feeling dizzy as she made her way back to her room. In the last year and a half she'd been living in Shattershard on and off, bunking off school or sneaking out of her house at night to spend time there, and the guild-house was a home away from home for her.

She liked the long dusty corridors leading back into the rock; the taciturn and secretive magicians left her alone as she did them and the libraries and reading rooms were just the sort of places she had hidden in before finding out about the Door Between Worlds. While at school her grades were indifferent to bad, here she'd got a reputation as an industrious student of magic, often doing apprentice work for the other guild-house magicians in exchange for their teaching her. While Laura and Alex had been getting a reputation for selling exotic merchandise, Morgan had kept quietly to the guild-house, only occasionally coming out into the city or joining the perpetual evening court at the palace.

That night when she let herself in to her tapestry-draped room, feeling the silence spells around her like a reassuring blanket of privacy, she'd stared at herself in the long swing-mirror at the side of her room, swirling around in a circle and looking flirtatiously from under her eyelashes at her reflection. Her own face looked back at her starry-eyed with amazement. Although she'd felt awkward and tongue-tied in the presence of the boy Archon, Kal hadn't seemed to mind. By the time she'd left him she'd been almost certain he was flirting with her.

Morgan changed into a black cotton night-shift and climbed into her four-poster bed, feeling like a princess in a story. It didn't even occur to her to remember her argument with Laura and Zoë or her strange encounter with Charm. Her mind was full of Kal as she fell easily into sleep. Like Kal's, her dreams were confused and absorbing.

But unlike him she didn't wake to the slow brightening of witch-light. Morgan surfaced from her dreams to a dark room and the growing certainty that there was someone there with her.

She struggled up from the bedclothes, crouching back against the pillows and searching with her left hand on the bedside table for the sharp little dagger that was the only weapon she owned.

'Illuminate,' she croaked with dry lips, concentrating her mind on the magic caged in the witch-lights, and to her relief they came alight.

Her suspicions had been correct. Facing her from the end of the bed were twin figures, dressed alike in magical black, staring at her with huge violet eyes.

'Don't be afraid,' Ciren said instantly as Morgan's hand closed on the hilt of the dagger. 'We won't hurt you.'

Morgan kept her eyes on him as she adjusted her position at the head of the bed, noticing only enough with her peripheral vision to see that Charm was wearing her short swords but not touching their hilts.

'Tell that to your sister,' she said, hearing her voice tremble as she spoke. 'She's the one who read my mind yesterday.'

'You could sense that?' Charm said suddenly, her voice sounding genuinely surprised rather than menacing.

'If you try anything I'll scream and I'll use all my magic against you,' Morgan said in a thin tight voice, her throat clenching up at the thought that the threat might not worry them. 'Please go away.'

'You don't have as much magic as you pretend to . . . ' Charm said, confirming her fears; but Ciren interrupted her.

'It's all right,' he said, keeping his eyes on Morgan. 'She won't read your mind if you'll agree to talk to us, I promise.' He flicked his eyes right and said, 'Promise her, Charm.'

'For now, I promise,' the girl said and Morgan risked a look at her. The girl mage's mouth was set in a grim line and she didn't look pleased about it but Morgan relaxed a little.

'What . . . what do you want to talk to me for?' she asked, looking back at Ciren, and the blond boy regarded her seriously.

'Because we know what you are.'

Morgan had leapt out of bed and backed right back to the wall, feeling the cold rock through the warmth of the tapestries, before she realized what she was doing. She could feel her heart pounding in shock as she stared at the twins. Neither of them came any nearer, although they both turned to face her, Charm now half-hidden behind Ciren.

'You come from a world with an alien magic,' the girl said quietly. 'Where men and women live in cities of hundreds upon thousands and make machines of metal to carry them across the ground and through the air and even children have toys that make the conjurings of magicians look paltry in comparison.' Her face stayed set in the same grim expression as she added, 'This is what I read from your mind.'

'Everything about you indicates a world-traveller,' Ciren said gently as Morgan continued to clutch her little dagger with shaking hands. 'This is something we've experience of.' His eyes made contact with hers as he said again, 'Please believe that you don't have to be afraid. My twin and I belong to an organization that exists to help and guide people like you.' He paused before asking gently, 'Have you never heard of the Collegiate?'

'No . . . ' Morgan shook her head. 'I've never heard of anything like that.' Her voice was still as shaky as her hands but her heartbeat was calming down as the two showed no sign of attacking.

Ciren took a step backwards to stand once more beside Charm and indicated them both with a sweeping gesture.

'Neither of us come from this world,' he said. 'Like many Collegiate members we are travellers, moving from Door to Door across the many worlds.' He reached to his neck and pulled out a black flinty arrowhead hung on a strip of leather from under his collar. 'This is a symbol of our organization.'

Morgan blinked at him and shifted the dagger from one hand to the other, wiping her sweaty palms on the side of her nightgown.

'Many worlds?' she asked uncertainly and Charm nodded.

'One of the duties of Collegiate members is to initiate world-travellers into our secrets,' she said. 'Many people who discover a Door into another world come to grief on the other side. Those who survive generally encounter a Collegiate member sooner or later. There are more worlds and more Doors than you could imagine possible. The Collegiate is the only organization that exists to protect those who travel between them.'

'I've never even heard about something like that,' Morgan objected nervously. 'And I've been studying magic ever since I first arrived here.'

Ciren shrugged fluidly and smiled at her.

'With respect, Shattershard is one small city state on the borders of a magical but not especially scholarly empire. This world has only really built itself up from barbarism in the last few generations. It's not surprising that you wouldn't know about the Collegiate. Very few cultures have any idea of the existence of Doors and Collegiate members are forbidden to reveal them to anyone who isn't a world-traveller.'

Despite her fear, Morgan was listening intently and she admitted to herself that the idea of a sort of unofficial police force for world travels didn't sound all that unlikely. Although she knew that Laura and Alex thought of Shattershard like Narnia, their own particular playpen, she had wondered for a long time if there could be more Doors into other worlds. As Ciren and Charm continued to explain, their voices alternating with a practised reasonableness, she realized slowly that she did believe them.

'So why are you telling me all this?' she asked eventually, keeping her hold on the dagger although she let the hand holding it rest at her side.

'Because it's our duty to,' Charm said coolly. 'Because as members of the Collegiate we're required to give you this information and render you any aid we can short of endangering our own well-being.'

Morgan frowned, trying to think that through, and thinking it sounded like the terminology of a legal contract or a social worker's care order. Ciren smiled again at her puzzlement and explained further.

'Because you're one of us,' he said. 'This is your initiation into the Collegiate.'

7

Coming back to Earth had felt like coming back to earth for Zoë. When she and Alex and Laura had come out of the woods and back into the Harrells' garden, seeing the beer cans and crisp packets lying around near the charred circle of the bonfire and the people still sleeping on the floor of the living room inside the house, it had been hard to believe the three of them had visited another world.

Picking her way through the detritus of last night's party, Zoë watched in surprise as Alex and Laura blithely ignored the mess.

'When are your parents getting back?' she asked, unable to help herself, and Laura looked bored.

'Some time today,' she said shrugging a shoulder at the debris. 'We'll get round to clearing up some time. It's not important.'

Laura stepped over the sleeping bodies and began making coffee in the kitchen and Zoë realized that Laura was simply not going to talk about Shattershard at all when she was in this world. Instead Zoë accepted a cup of coffee and drank it slowly while Alex went to get his car.

She'd passed through tiredness into the sort of achy-eyed alertness you got when you'd had no sleep but you had to get up in the morning. The pale English sunshine wasn't bright enough to hurt her eyes compared to the dazzling sun of the desert and she stood in the doorway of the house sipping her coffee as Alex drove a small Audi around from the side of the house. Rolling down the window, Alex left the engine running as he called, 'Get in.'

Zoë hurriedly looked for somewhere to put the mug and found Laura taking it out of her hands.

'Take care,' she said, smiling and Zoë grinned back awkwardly.

'Thanks,' she said, glancing apologetically at Alex for the delay. 'Um, I had a really amazing time.' She winced at her own awkwardness and Laura laughed.

'See you soon,' she said and walked with Zoë to the car.

'Shall I get anything for you while I'm out?' Alex asked Laura as Zoë got into the passenger seat.

Surprised at the question, Zoë watched while Laura thought for a moment and then produced a list.

'Stationery would be good,' she said. 'Some more of those A2 rolls of paper and blank bound notebooks, the kind that's sewn not stuck.'

Alex nodded and rolled the window back up and Zoë waved goodbye awkwardly one last time as the car set off down the drive. As Alex drove down the slope of Bicken Hill and round a small roundabout to get on to the ring road Zoë stared out of the window at the cars going past as if she were in a foreign country.

'Where do you live anyway?' Alex asked and Zoë glanced across at him.

'At the army base,' she said. 'I came to your party with some of the guys you know from the base.'

'Oh, right.' Alex looked back at her with a sort of surprised recognition. 'I do remember now. Your parents are in the army?'

'My dad is,' Zoë said, feeling uncomfortable as she always did when people asked her about where she lived. 'He's a major.'

'Oh, really?' Alex looked at her again and Zoë wished he'd keep his eyes on the road. If she felt this dazed and hungover he must be too.

'Yeah,' she said, looking away and out of the window. 'You know where the base is, right?'

'I know where it is,' Alex said. 'Do I need some kind of pass to get in?'

'It's OK, you can drop me at the gate,' Zoë said and looked back just in time to catch him looking disappointed.

When Alex dropped her, Zoë waited until he'd gone before going back into the base. She didn't want any of the squaddies to see him leaving her and make comments about where she'd been last night. She fumbled in her bag for her base pass, feeling worried for a second when she couldn't put her fingers on it before taking a deep breath when she felt it in the corner of her bag.

As usual the guy on duty hardly noticed as she showed it to him and she walked quickly towards her house. When a voice suddenly called her name she jumped and it was with relief that she recognized Dan Siefer jogging towards her.

'Zoë!' he called, coming quickly to join her. 'Where were you? We couldn't find you when we left and some guy said you'd gone off with Laura. Chris was kind of pissed off about it when you didn't show up.'

'Yeah.' Zoë felt awkward. 'I must have missed you looking for me. Sorry about that.'

Dan looked disappointed and Zoë realized that he might have been hoping she'd wanted to be with him at the party. A day ago that would have been enough to make her feel happy and excited but now her head was just too full of the things she'd discovered and she took a few steps on down the path to try and get away.

'So where did you go, anyway?' Dan insisted. 'You know we could have got into trouble if you didn't show up.'

'I'm fine, Dan,' Zoë said. 'I just fell asleep in a corner. Laura's brother drove me back.'

'Oh.' Dan's face fell and Zoë blushed a little at the idea of what he might assume from that but didn't try to correct him.

'Look, I'll see you, OK,' she said, taking a few more steps away. 'Thanks for the ride to the party.'

'See you,' she heard Dan say behind her as she headed up the little path to her front door and let herself in.

Inside, the little house was just as she'd left it. Her own note to her father was stuck to the fridge and she crumpled it up and threw it away before going up to her room. Catching a glimpse of herself in the mirror she paused to search her own eyes for any sign that she'd changed and her reflection looked guiltily back. Suddenly determined to get back to normal she changed quickly and winced when she saw the little pile of sand that had shaken loose from her clothes. Wrapping herself in her dressing-gown she swept it up with her hands and was about to drop it in the bin when she changed her mind and put it into a little wooden box instead, hiding it away in one of her desk drawers.

Once she'd showered and changed into jeans and a plain top, plaiting her hair back and scrunchying it tightly behind her head, she began to feel more normal. It was Saturday afternoon and her dad wasn't expected back until the next day but Zoë couldn't think of anything she wanted to do. She could have gone into Weybridge town centre and seen if there was anyone from school hanging out at the mall. That was what she usually did during school holidays but now it just seemed irredeemably pathetic. She wondered about phoning Laura but couldn't convince herself to pick up the receiver, not sure what she would say. Instead she mooched about the house aimlessly for a while and went for a walk around the base, coming back when she saw Dan Siefer and his brother playing basketball with some friends on the recreation ground.

She still wasn't ready to start thinking about her experiences in the other world and she made pizza for dinner, eating in front of the television and watching her way through two episodes of *The Simpsons*, a celebrity talk show, and the first half of a kids' film she'd seen last year. When she was too tired to keep her eyes open properly she gave it up and clicked off the TV set. It was dark outside and she closed the curtains belatedly, shivering a little in the cold house, and went upstairs to her bedroom. Suddenly she wished more than anything that her dad would come home.

Major Sam Kaul might have to leave his daughter on her own more than he'd have preferred but he was a generous dad. When he got back on Sunday evening to the smell of casserole cooking in the little kitchen he dropped his bags in the hall and called for Zoë. When she hurried out to hug him he ruffled her hair and gave her a tight bear-hug.

'You cooked, Zozo?' he said, coming into the kitchen and bending to look at the casserole cooking in the oven. 'You must have missed me! I thought I'd be lucky if I could rustle up some cold pizza.'

'I ate all the pizza,' Zoë said, grinning at him happily and pushing him back into the living room. 'You should sit down. Did you have a good trip?'

'You're sure I can't help?' her dad said and then stopped her when she was about to go back to the kitchen. 'Hang on, soldier. At ease! I brought you a present. Close your eyes and open your hands.'

'Dad!' Zoë said, rolling her eyes in pretend embarrassment at the old pet-name before shutting them and squinting through her eyelashes as he dropped a heavy item into her arms. It was a coat made of soft cream-coloured leather with epaulets and a huge dramatically folded over collar and Zoë looked at it with amazement.

'It's gorgeous,' she said reverentially. 'But it must have cost hundreds of pounds, Dad!'

'Glad you like it,' her dad said, getting a beer from the kitchen and opening it as she tried the coat on and looked down at herself admiringly. 'Suits you, too. But it didn't exactly break the bank. I saw some kids on the base over there wearing them and thought of you. Leather doesn't cost nearly as much over there.'

'I love it,' Zoë assured him. 'I bet no one at school has anything like it.'

'You'll knock their socks off,' her dad said. 'So how was the big last day? Any excitement?'

Zoë hesitated at that and used the excuse of checking on the casserole to escape for a minute. She'd spent all day waiting for and wanting her dad to come home so she could talk to him about what had happened to her but now she knew she couldn't do it. If she tried to tell him she'd been into another world he'd think she was making it up and if she insisted he'd be worried she was going crazy. A girl at one of the places they'd lived before had been mad like that, insisting that people were following her around

122

in unmarked cars, and the school counsellor had told her parents it was because they left her alone too much. Zoë couldn't bear the thought of her dad thinking she'd lost it because of his being away.

As she served up casserole and baked potatoes on to plates she was aware that she'd almost forgotten Alex and Laura's insistence that the Door Between Worlds was a secret. With a sinking feeling she realized she didn't really trust them. All the time she'd been with them they'd acted as if Shattershard was their world, their own private kingdom, and now she thought about it that seemed wrong to her.

'Dinner is served,' she announced, carrying the plates through to the dining table and her dad inhaled appreciatively, admiring the table setting and the small vase of flowers she'd put there.

'Looks delicious,' he said. 'Tell you what, I'll open some wine for us seeing as it's a special occasion.'

It wasn't until halfway through dinner that Zoë's dad brought up the subject of the last day of term again and Zoë decided to compromise on a half truth.

'A kind of strange thing happened,' she said slowly and her dad looked at her searchingly.

'Strange like *X-Files* strange or strange like getting-into-trouble-Dad-won't-like strange?' he asked and Zoë bit her lip.

'Well, like, maybe both sort of,' she said, trying to explain. 'I went to a party on Friday night.'

'Mmm-hmm,' her dad said, waiting for her to cut to the chase.

'Dan Siefer invited me,' Zoë said quickly. 'He lives three doors down, you know? I left a note in case you got back early.'

'Very responsible, soldier,' her dad said drily. 'Was it the kind of party I'd have approved of?'

'It was on Bicken Hill,' Zoë told him. 'At the house of a girl in my class, although it was mostly her brother's friends there.' She paused. 'Their parents weren't around.'

'Uh-huh. Did you drink?'

'A beer I didn't finish and some wine,' Zoë said, knowing what was coming next.

'Did you take drugs?'

'No, not even weed,' she said hastily and her dad frowned.

'There's no ''not even'' about it, Zoë,' he said. 'I don't want you taking any drugs.'

'I don't, Daddy,' Zoë said, feeling oddly reassured to be having this familiar conversation even though her dad was looking stern. 'I was just saying that if I did, weed's not as bad as some stuff, right?'

'On a scale of things that would get you grounded for the next month it's not that bad,' he agreed in a reasonable tone of voice. 'But it's still not allowed.' He paused to let that sink in and then smiled before asking, 'So what was the weird thing that happened?'

Zoë had already decided what she was going to say and the lie came out easily. She was used to changing her stories about things when she met new people at school, shifting the details of her life to make them seem more glamorous or more mundane depending on her audience. She even sometimes lied to her dad although she tried not to. She had tried drugs once and fortunately he hadn't asked her about it afterwards and she hadn't admitted it since. But she mostly kept to his rules since he was always willing to discuss them with her. Now she was hoping she could get some advice from him.

Putting down her fork and knife she took a little drink of her wine and told the version of the story she'd been preparing.

'This girl whose house the party was at is called Laura,' she began.

'I think I've seen her,' her dad said thoughtfully. 'Was she one of the kids roped into handing out name-tags at that parents' night last month?'

'Um, yeah, maybe,' Zoë said, surprised. 'Everyone knows Laura, Dad. She's like omnipresent or something. She's not popular but . . .'

'She's accepted?' her dad said and Zoë nodded.

'Exactly. Like she fits in wherever she wants to. Well, she and I got to talking at the party and I think,' she hesitated, 'I think that we're friends now.'

'That's good, isn't it?' Her dad had finished his own meal and was sitting back in his chair watching her as he drank some of his wine. 'I know you've been on the lookout for a new best friend.'

'Yeah . . .' Zoë said, feeling a pang as she thought about it. That had been all she'd wanted from Laura originally and now she was just too confused about the other world to really know what she thought about the other girl. 'But the thing is that she . . . Laura and her brother have this game they play.'

'Yes?' Her dad frowned and Zoë bit her lip, choosing her words carefully.

'It's sort of geeky really, it's a role-playing game. They pretend that they have this whole other world that they can visit. Sort of like Narnia. And they make up stories and things about it.'

Zoë's dad poured himself some more wine and then refilled her glass a little before sitting down again, thinking about it.

'Well, that is a little strange at their age,' he said. 'But a lot of people are into strategy games, aren't they? Do they have a map of the world they visit and tokens for armies?'

'Uh . . . yeah,' Zoë said, thinking quickly. 'They have this map of a city that's on the edge of a desert and there are these nomads outside and a sort of empire that's kind of in charge of it all.'

'Sounds fun,' her dad said. 'So what do you think? Did Laura and her brother invite you to play?'

'Yeah, and it was fun,' Zoë said quickly. 'But it's like . . . like Laura's a different person when she's playing the game. She's really intense about it and I think if I'm going to be her friend I'm going to get into it myself.'

'Well, that's OK by me,' her dad said. 'You know the rules. So long as you're back by curfew and let me know where you are, you can go and play role-playing games to your heart's content.'

Zoë felt a sudden lump in her throat and had to take a sip of wine to disguise it. Suddenly, lying to her dad felt like the worst thing she'd ever done and she wondered what kind of person she was to trick him like this.

'What's wrong, Zozo?' he said softly. 'Do you think this game is a bit too much for you, is that it?'

'Maybe,' Zoë said, not looking at him and scuffing one of her feet under the table. 'But maybe I just don't feel like I really understand what's going on. I mean, this other world is really complicated.'

'Sounds like your new friends have dropped you in a bit out of your depth,' her dad said seriously and Zoë looked up in surprise. He had a thoughtful look that made her feel comforted. Zoë knew her dad was intelligent. Maybe even without telling him the whole truth he could come up with something that would help her decide how she felt about all this.

'Zoë, you're a clever girl,' he said after a while. 'And you've managed to make a difficult situation work for you here. You're good at working out what's expected of you and adapting to new circumstances.' He smiled at her. 'I honestly don't think there's much that will faze you but it's inevitable as you grow up that you'll find yourself having to make some difficult decisions about people.'

Zoë felt and must have looked confused because her dad held up a hand for a second, indicating that she should let him finish.

'We all try to fit in,' he said. 'A good soldier follows orders because he's been trained to respond to a chain of command. A good citizen obeys the law even when he disagrees with some of its provisions.' He paused before saying, 'You've always been good at working out the rules, Zoë. But sometimes it's important to remember that whatever rules we obey we do so by choice.' He grinned suddenly and added, 'That goes for my rules for you, as well . . . although that's not an encouragement to go out and start breaking them!'

'OK . . . ' Zoë said thinking it through. 'So you're saying that I should play the game if I want to but that I don't have to do what Laura and Alex say in it?'

'Well, if they're teaching you the game you probably do have to play by their rules,' her dad said with a smile. 'But you're free to make up your own mind what you think about them.'

They washed up the dinner dishes together afterwards and Zoë thought to herself about what her dad had said about Laura and Alex. It was true that she'd felt out of her depth in Shattershard but his comments about her ability to adjust to new situations had made her start thinking seriously about the things she'd seen there. More than anything else what stood out was the difference between the two factions of the Tetrarchate and the Hajhim.

It wasn't until she'd explained the background to her dad that she'd really noticed how different the two cultures were. In the shops and markets of Shattershard the people had been of a wide variety of types from fair-skinned to dark-skinned and in radically different cultural costumes. But in the palace the people had been exclusively Caucasian types: fair-skinned, light-haired, and mainly blue- or grey-eyed; unlike the black-haired brown-eyed Hajhim she'd left the city with. Alex was obviously involved with Jhezra and Laura had admitted that she was working some arrangement with the Hajhi servants at her mansion to get them into the city somehow.

The more Zoë thought about it, it was clear that Laura and Alex were on the side of the Hajhim despite the fact that the rest of the city people seemed to be against them, and she remembered again Dan's brother saying that Alex had a 'dictator complex'.

'Laura's brother is really into war, Dad,' she said, pulling the plug out of the sink for the water to drain out. 'I think he'd like to be a soldier. Laura said his hero is Lawrence of Arabia.'

'T. E. Lawrence?' Her dad glanced across at her. 'He was more of a hero than a soldier. The British army never really forgave him for going native.'

'Going native?' Zoë asked and her dad shrugged.

'It's slang for prioritizing the local culture over your own people,' he said and when Zoë looked at him he raised his hands. 'It's not something I necessarily agree with,' he said. 'But remember when we talked about double agents and how they're mistrusted by both sides? Going native's something like that. A lot of people see it as a betrayal.' He paused and added, 'Lawrence wasn't ever completely accepted by the Arabs, you know. Everyone's a product of their own culture, no matter how hard they try to see the other point of view.'

When they'd finished washing up, Zoë asked if she could call Laura and her dad told her to go ahead. She found the

Harrells on Bicken Hill easily in the local directory but there was no answer on the phone. She waited, counting to twenty rings before she hung up, and then went back to join her dad in the living room. 'Buck up, soldier,' he said. 'You can try her again tomorrow.' But the next morning there was still no answer on the phone.

Zoë's dad took the day off on Monday and they went shopping in the city centre where Zoë bought a pair of grey combats with her allowance and a blank notebook from W. H. Smith. Her dad had his hair cut while they shopped and afterwards they had lunch at a local restaurant. When she got home she tried phoning Laura again but there was still no answer. Feeling frustrated, Zoë sat in her room and wondered what to do. She really wanted to see Laura again and to find out more about the Door Between Worlds. It seemed that every five minutes she thought of another question about it and about Shattershard and she remembered Laura's promise that there would be a next time with increasing excitement as her worries of the weekend faded.

After dinner that night she tried to call Laura three more times but still no one picked up the phone. Sitting in the front hall, Zoë fiddled with the corner of the phone directory and then slowly turned to the letter M. There were more than twenty Michaelses in the book and she put it down again, telling herself that calling Morgan was a stupid idea anyway. Then she remembered the class schedule book she'd been given at the beginning of term and went quickly back up to her room to look for it. She found it at the bottom of a drawer. She'd never used it, despite the fact that it had pages for a diary and a list to write down homework assignments, because everyone at school despised the things. However, in the front there were class lists for everyone in her year and Morgan was listed.

Zoë dialled the number slowly, her hands sweaty on the receiver. Calling Morgan probably wasn't a good idea but she needed someone to talk to. After only five rings someone picked up the phone and a man's voice said, 'Yes?'

'Um,' Zoë felt panicked and it took her a couple of seconds to find words. 'Can I speak to Morgan, please?'

'She's not here,' the voice said brusquely but before Zoë could apologize or hang up someone else took over the phone.

'Who is this?' asked a sharp female voice and Zoë wished she hadn't called.

'This is Zoë,' she said. 'Is that Morgan?'

'I'm her *mum*, right?' the voice said and Zoë blushed. 'Morgan's not here,' it continued in an annoyed tone. 'She's not been back in days and if you see her you can tell that little madam from me she's knee-deep in shit, orright?'

'Look, I'm sorry but I really don't know her very well,' Zoë tried to say but Morgan's mother wasn't listening.

'If she ain't back tonight tell her she'll be out on her ear, orright?' the voice said again loudly. 'You listening to that, madam? You get back here or else!'

'Sorry,' Zoë said again and then, unable to think of what else to do, she hung up the phone.

For several minutes afterwards she waited by it in case Morgan's mum did 1471 and phoned her back but when nothing happened she went back to her room. She tried Laura's number once more that night, checking it against the version in her class book, but there was still no answer and on Tuesday when her dad left for work she decided to try a different approach. Leaving the base and walking down the road she found a bus stop with signs to Bicken Hill and waited for half an hour until the bus arrived.

It took another half hour for the bus to wend its way

through Weybridge and up the smart streets of Bicken Hill and Zoë spent the time staring out of the window at the town. No wonder Laura didn't have any real friends here, she thought, when she spent all her free time in somewhere like Shattershard. Uncomfortably she remembered her conversation with Morgan's mother and wondered if the black-haired girl had been in Shattershard ever since the weekend. It seemed callous to go off and not come home even though Morgan's mum had kind of scared her.

Although Zoë had checked the address in her class book it took a while for her to find Laura's house amid the curving streets of Bicken Hill. Eventually she located it by aiming for the edge of the Weywode Forest she could see to her left and finally finding the dirt track that Dan's brother had followed the other night. At the end of the road was the Harrells' house and she recognized the sprawling garden as she approached. At the front of the house a middle-aged woman was raking up autumn leaves into an untidy heap on the drive and she looked up as Zoë came through the gate.

'Hi,' Zoë said awkwardly. 'Um. I'm a friend of Laura's. Is she around?'

'It's more polite to say your name first,' the woman said, straightening up from her raking and looking Zoë over. She had grey-brown hair in an untidy bun at the back of her neck and cold watery blue eyes behind thick-lensed glasses.

'I'm Zoë,' Zoë said. 'Zoë Kaul. I'm in Laura's class at school.'

'Well, Zoë. First you say "How do you do, Mrs Harrell",' the woman said in the same cool tone as before. 'Then you introduce yourself and ask if you may see Laura.'

Zoë gritted her teeth. Even Morgan's mother hadn't been as bad as this.

'Good morning, Mrs Harrell,' she said deliberately. 'How do you do? May I please see Laura, if she's available?'

'She's out,' Laura's mother said in the same tone of voice but Zoë thought she sounded triumphant. 'Perhaps you should consider phoning first.'

Mrs Harrell criticized her manners twice more before Zoë managed to escape and she left the garden beginning to feel as if she had an idea why Laura liked to spend so much time in Shattershard. But once she was out of the woman's view she didn't feel like going back home. Without really acknowledging what she was doing she walked on down to the edge of the dirt track around the back of the Harrells' garden and discovered a path into the Weywode Forest by a sign reading: 'Public Footpath and Nature Walk'.

Zoë went on, climbing over a stile when the forest started and following the footpath for about five minutes. Then, when it began to curve down the hill, she turned away from the track and worked her way back towards the edge of the Harrells' garden. On Friday night Laura had taken her through a gate from that garden and into Weywode Forest. Now, during the day, Zoë tried to work out what that path had been.

It took a while. Despite herself she was nervous of losing her way, even though she kept careful track of the path she had taken and the position of the Harrells' house behind her. When she came upon a thinly worn footpath she thought it seemed familiar but it took some working out to see its turns and twists through the trees. However, when she came to a small clearing the location was unmistakable. During the day the splotch of darkness beneath the trees could be distinguished easily and Zoë walked up to it wonderingly. Seeing the Door for the first time on her own made her nervous and she glanced instinctively over her shoulder, not knowing what she feared.

When she looked back the Door was still there, unchanged. Walking slowly towards it Zoë stretched out her hand and touched it to the complete blackness. Her fingers sank through a little and she flinched instinctively before putting her other hand up and through into the darkness. Nothing felt different, just as it hadn't the other day, and taking a deep breath Zoë stepped through the Door Between Worlds.

8

On the other side of the Door it was dark. Her eyes widening instinctively, Zoë put out her hands, feeling for something, and barked her knuckles painfully on rock. For a second she had panicked that something had gone wrong with the Door, trapping her between worlds, before she looked up and saw beyond the shadowing shapes of the rocks around her to the stars brightening the sky above.

Feeling her way round the side of the rock scree Zoë climbed down the ragged rocks towards the sandy floor of the desert. Ahead down the road she could see the vast bulk of the city of Shattershard and even make out lights burning on the topmost towers of the mountain, but all around the sandy plain was dark and featureless. She shivered a bit in the cold air. Her clothes were warm enough for the end of English autumn but in the middle of the desert night she felt gooseflesh on her arms and the rocks were cold as ice.

Harness jingled suddenly, ringing out across the stillness of the desert and Zoë hunkered down quickly next to the nearest rocks. Coming along the road towards the city was a troop of soldiers: at least twenty of them, riding horses and armed with swords. Their eyes searched the darkness on either side of them as they rode along. Hiding in the rocks at the side of the road, Zoë realized she had made a mistake. She should never have come through the Door so unprepared. But while the troop of soldiers was going down the road she didn't dare move.

Wiggling further back into the shadows she caught the heel of her foot and a scatter of pebbles bounced down to the road. One of the soldiers reined in his horse a little and turned to look over his shoulder, staring directly at the place where Zoë was hidden. She held her breath, trying not to move a muscle, but he continued to stare, his hand going to the sword at his belt. Beside him another rider slowed and asked a question but, although Zoë was wearing the translation amulet Laura had bought her, she couldn't make out the words. Her whole body was tense, the sand rough on her arms and legs and her muscles cramping in her awkward crouch. Then the first soldier shrugged and turned away, the two trotting their horses to move back into line with the rest of the troop.

Zoë watched them depart, her heart still in her mouth, only shifting enough to get rid of the worst of her cramp as the jingle of harness faded up the winding road ahead. When they were finally out of sight she stood up slowly and took a shuddering deep breath.

'Who are you?' a voice demanded from behind her.

Whirling, Zoë turned to see a tall girl dressed in a sand-coloured tunic and trousers. For a second Zoë thought it was Jhezra but this girl's black hair was chopped roughly short to her head and her eyes were narrow and hostile. She carried a curved sword at her belt and in her right hand held a similarly curved dagger and as Zoë stared at her she gestured with it impatiently.

'Who are you?' she said again. 'And what are you doing here?'

'I'm . . . I'm a traveller,' Zoë stammered and the girl curled her lip contemptuously.

'No one is fool enough to travel alone in the desert at night,' she said. 'You were hiding from the soldiers. Why?'

'You were hiding from them too!' Zoë said hotly. 'Or else you wouldn't have seen me.'

'If I was it's none of your concern,' the girl told her. 'And it wasn't me who they heard. You're obviously not one of us, so what are you doing here?'

'I . . . ' Zoë hesitated and the girl's hand strayed to the hilt of her scimitar warningly. 'I was looking for friends of mine,' Zoë said quickly.

'What sort of friends of yours would be wandering the desert?'

Zoë thought quickly. Being caught by this girl wasn't as frightening as the thought of being seen by the blue and silver soldiers had been. Although she was obviously a Hajhi warrior this girl didn't seem much older than Zoë herself and she was on her own. But even so, Zoë didn't want to annoy her, so she said the only thing she could.

'They have friends from your people,' she said. 'They're called Alex and Laura. You might know them yourself.'

The girl shook her head.

'I don't know those names,' she said. 'You'll have to try harder than that if you want to convince me.'

'They're friends of Jhezra's,' Zoë tried again. 'Do you know Jhezra?'

She didn't have to ask. The first time she'd said the name the girl's expression had changed and now she lowered the point of her dagger.

'I know Jhezra,' she admitted. 'Tell me the names of these others again.'

'Laura and Alexander,' Zoë said. 'Alex is Jhezra's friend.'

The girl cocked her head on one side suddenly and said, 'Iskander? Is that who you mean?'

'Tall, curly dark hair, wears a long brown coat?' Zoë said, relaxing now. 'He's Laura's brother. I'm Laura's friend.'

'I'm Vaysha.' The girl slung her dagger back on her belt and put her hands together in the same gesture Jhezra had used when they first met. Zoë mirrored the movement, bowing a little over her hands before smiling at Vaysha.

'Pleased to meet you,' she said carefully, letting her relief show. 'I guess it was pretty stupid of me to come here at night.'

While Zoë was receiving a first-hand lesson in the dangers of the desert, the Tetrarchic troop she had seen on the road was circling to the west of the city. They were not the only patrol out that night and twice they stopped on the road to exchange words with other troops similarly engaged. Zoë would have been disturbed to know that the soldier who had almost spotted her had mentioned thinking he saw something in the rocks to a friend from another patrol heading off in that direction. Tetrarchic soldiers were trained to be paranoid.

From the guard and gate towers of the mountain city the Shattershard militia shared an uneasy watch with their Tetrarchate counterparts. Normally guard duty was a relaxed affair, despite the recent losses of the caravans; from the high towers you could see for miles across the desert during the day and hear for miles at night. The guards usually whiled away the long watches of the night in idle conversation and with a few warming draughts of beer or flasks of wine. But tonight they stood at attention, their eyes shifting only briefly from the desert to meet those of their friends, while the Tetrarchic soldiers stood on watch with bows ready strung, some using spyglasses to watch the desert. Shattershard was a city under martial law and the local guards didn't much like the experience.

They weren't alone in that feeling. The court that night at the palace was just as uneasy, nerves highly strung and voices highly pitched as they discussed recent events in the city. While Zoë had spent a mundane weekend in Weybridge, Shattershard had not stayed unchanged. It had been three days since General Shirishath's troops had joined the city guard at the gate, refusing entry to any of the Hajhim who attempted to pass them. Two days ago the Archon had stood up in front of the court to tell them that the Tetrarch had ordered the pacification of the Hajhim and that Shattershard had no choice but to co-operate. Just the day before, the largest caravan of merchants for months had passed through the city gates. With the merchants had gone the last of the people who feared the coming battle: the ill, the cowardly, the pacifists, and the superstitious.

The courtiers were as elegantly dressed as always but there were fewer of them now. Some black-clad magicians had remained and talked in huddled groupings around the edges of the stairways and balconies. The older priests travelled with an entourage of acolytes, armed with ceremonial weapons, and were strung with so many charms and icons that they clattered as they walked. In contrast the noblemen and women, those that had not gone on convenient visits to distant relations, wore less jewellery than usual. Most of their assets were locked in safe places and strongboxes in their mansions or had gone to pay their own bodyguards. Throughout the crowd the remaining merchants did brisk business, bartering and bargaining to get high prices for the few supplies left in the city.

In the Audience Hall Shattershard's Archon watched his subjects quietly. Beside him on the dais the ranks of his own advisers had diminished, although Jagannath still sat by his side.

'Trade has slowed to a trickle,' Kal said softly. 'Over half the city's residences are unoccupied.' His voice dropped even further as he added: 'People are afraid.'

'General Shirishath reports that for the last two days no Hajhim have attempted to enter the gate and his patrols have caught no sight of them in the immediate vicinity of the city,' Jagannath reminded him. 'Perhaps the nomads have decided to abandon the conflict?'

'Perhaps,' Kal said. But looking around the virtually empty hall he doubted it. Shattershard had the feel of tension building before a storm. The Hajhim had forced this confrontation; they weren't likely to back off without a fight. 'Do you believe that, Jagannath?' he asked. 'Truly?'

The cardinal met his eyes with a small shake of his head.

'In truth I don't know what I believe, my Archon,' he said. 'But I fear.' He leant closer, despite the fact that they were already speaking too quietly to be overheard by any of the distant courtiers. 'Shirishath is confident but he doesn't know as well as we do how cunning the Hajhim have grown.' He paused. 'Many of the aristocracy have left the city, Lord Archon. Perhaps for the sake of your health . . .'

'No.' Kal shook his head abruptly. 'While the city stands and there is any one of the people left inside . . .' He shook his head again. 'You told me before I had enemies, Jagannath. Not the Hajhim. But whoever has brought this conflict to this point. This is what they've been working for. Even if I can't defeat them, I want to look them in the face.'

The cardinal studied his expression, looking as if he would have liked to protest against Kal's decision, but he said nothing and at last he nodded. Since the declaration of martial law Kal's authority over the city was next to nothing but the boy Archon had been trained since the moment of his birth to believe in his duty and they both knew that if he left the city now he would never be accepted back.

Standing, Kal stepped down from the Archon's throne, nodding in response to the bows of the courtiers as he left the hall. From the doorway Athen and Edren stepped to follow him as he made his way through the public rooms. As he walked, people stopped to bow to him but Kal didn't stop for more than a moment to exchange greetings or sample any of the lavish dishes and drinks being offered by the remaining servants. Instead he followed the curves of a staircase back into the interior of the palace, away from the public areas and towards the secluded garden where he was spending more and more of his time. At the arched doorway he paused.

'If you would wait here for me,' he said, glancing at his bodyguards.

'As you wish, Lord Archon,' Athen said, bowing, and Edren mimicked the motion.

'And . . . ' Kal hesitated and then said more slowly, 'I'd appreciate it if you could prevent me from being disturbed . . . ' The slightest suggestion of a smile crossed Athen's face and Kal smiled back. 'Unless it's urgent,' he added and Edren smiled as well.

'Of course, my lord, Kal. You can depend on us,' he said, taking up his post at the door.

Thanking them both again, Kal left them at the door

and went out into the night-time garden. He knew why
they had forgotten decorum so far as to smile but he didn't
blame them. With the current state of the city it was a
wonder that any of them had anything to smile at. Now,
with pale light illuminating the roof garden, he crossed
to the figure sitting waiting by the central fountain and
touched her shoulder gently, smiling when she turned
with a sudden blush.

'Hello again,' she said smiling and blushing at once as
he bent to put his arms around her.

'Hello, Morgan,' he said and kissed her.

In the public areas of the palace Kal's early disappearance
from the festivities hadn't gone unnoticed. Since gossip
was the only distraction from the imminent threat of war,
Trebbern the merchant was especially eager to speculate
on the reasons for Kal's absence.

'There's a rumour the young Archon has a secret lover,'
he said, trying to interest the person next to him in the
scandal. 'Unfortunately, his bodyguards are notoriously
discreet.'

'Really?' the young woman next to him said politely,
but her light-green eyes were faintly bored. 'Perhaps he's
consoling himself since there's nothing he can do about
the war.'

'Honestly, Laura,' Trebbern said, affronted. 'You are a
ghoul sometimes. Can't you think about anything except
war?'

'Was that an insult, Trebbern?' Laura's brother said,
appearing suddenly from behind them, and the plump
merchant jumped a bit in surprise.

'Oh no,' he said hastily. 'Certainly not. The lady Laura
knows how much I admire her.' Seeing Laura's empty
wine glass he seized on it and added quickly, 'Allow me to

express my apologies by fetching you another, my dear.' Then, before she could answer, he twinkled off.

Once the merchant was safely out of sight Alex leant down so Laura could take his arm and escorted her to an alcove out of the way where they could watch the crowd without being noticed.

'Did that idiot Trebbern know anything worthwhile?' he asked and Laura shrugged.

'He's an incurable gossip but he doesn't really know anything. Cardinal Jagannath and General Shirishath apparently argue every time they meet but that's unsurprising. And the boy-king has given up trying to govern and has found himself a girlfriend instead.'

'A girlfriend?' Alex was surprised into laughing. 'I didn't know he had it in him. Who is she?'

'Only the bodyguards know and they're not saying,' Laura said casually. 'What about you? What have you heard?'

'Nothing useful,' Alex told her and his face shifted into a frown. 'I'm not really very good at this.'

Despite himself he was worried. Even though he still had free passage in and out of the city gates, he and Jhezra had decided that he should visit the desert only when it was strictly necessary. The Tetrarchic troops weren't stupid and now that the Hajhim weren't allowed into the city they would be on the lookout for spies. Faced with the alternatives of sitting at home in the residence and brooding over their plans or coming with Laura to court, he'd chosen the second option. But he didn't have Laura's knack for drawing other people out and he'd become too used to the casual camaraderie among the Hajhi warriors to enjoy the luxurious frivolity of the Archon's court.

Now he stood as Laura's escort and watched as she spoke to the passing courtiers, admiring the way she managed to flatter information out of some of them and steal it from others by pretending to know more than she did. It was a method that had worked well for them ever since they first arrived in Shattershard and although the other merchants had never guessed it, it was thanks to Laura that the Hajhim had such uncanny knowledge of when the caravans were travelling and what they carried. But tonight there wasn't much information to be gained and he was relieved when Laura finally suggested they go home.

Home meant their mansion residence at the moment. Ever since the martial law edict, they'd been spending half their time in Shattershard, only coming back to Weybridge in Earth's evening for long enough for their parents not to register them as missing. The Hajhi plan depended too much on them for Alex to want to go back at all but it couldn't be helped. If all went well they might stay in Shattershard for good but they couldn't risk the kind of complications that would come from the Weybridge police listing them as runaways.

It wasn't until they had reached the mansion, letting themselves in through its imposing double doors, that they could speak freely. While Laura brought a mirror from somewhere and set it up in front of her, taking off her make-up carefully, Alex made them coffee from their carefully hoarded stock.

'How was Jhezra today?' Laura asked and Alex shook his head.

'Worried,' he admitted. 'The plan was prepared with only Shattershard's militia in mind. The Hajhim can't help but be concerned now there are five hundred Tetrarchic troopers to contend with.'

'But they still intend to go ahead?' Laura asked quickly and Alex glanced at her.

They'd both been promised all sorts of rewards when the Hajhim took over the city but that had never concerned

Alex. The reward he was after was leading an army to victory. But Laura felt differently. The mansion they lived in and the Hajhi servants they pretended to employ had been her idea and he suspected she had just as many inspirations about what she'd do when Shattershard was being run by the Hajhim. Even though he knew she was on his side Alex sometimes wished she had a more poetic attitude towards their war instead of the mercenary interest of the merchant she pretended to be.

'They haven't changed their minds,' Alex said. 'It would be impossible to convince them to stop now even if we wanted to. The warriors are furious at the way the Tetrarchate troops have prevented them from going where they want in their desert. With the weapons we've helped them make, they're confident they can bring their part of the plan off.'

'And what about your part?' Laura asked. 'Originally you were supposed to have people to help you. How can you work it now the Hajhim aren't being allowed inside Shattershard?'

'Jhezra has an idea for that,' Alex told her. 'It's you I'm worried about. If the worst comes to the worst I can defend myself. I've got pretty good with a scimitar. But what are you going to do when we cut to the chase?'

'I'll go to the palace,' Laura said easily. 'It'll be the best guarded place in the city and by the time the Hajhim get around to taking it over, you can come and find me there.' She put down the cotton wool she was using to clean her make-up off and turned to give Alex a smile. 'It's ironic,' she said. 'The Tetrarchate troops themselves will be protecting me, until we're in control.'

Alex blinked at that but he couldn't think of any good reason to object to the plan so he went on to the next question.

'The Archon will be in the palace too,' he said. 'It

seems clear that he intends to stay until the bitter end. Remember to steer clear of him. If he realizes you're a spy . . . '

'I'll be careful,' Laura promised and Alex thought of something else.

'If he survives the battle I don't want to have him executed,' he said uncomfortably. 'Once we've taken over the city we should send him off to the Tetrarchate, don't you think?'

'Yes, why not?' Laura agreed. 'It'll make the Hajhim look good to let him go.' She paused. 'It's not Prince Kal I'm worried about. It's Morgan.'

'Morgan?' Alex said. 'Isn't she still playing with her magic somewhere in the guild-house?'

'So I've figured,' Laura agreed. 'But I told you about the threats she made at the palace. She's turned into a real bitch ever since she guessed what we were up to.'

'She doesn't know the details though,' Alex said. 'And she promised not to tell about us.' He hesitated. 'You're right though, it is a problem. And I don't think this was the best time to bring that other girl in either.'

'Zoë?' Laura smiled at him. 'Zoë's not a problem.' She smiled suddenly up at Alex. 'She practically worships me and she has no idea what we're doing here.' She made a dismissive gesture, brushing a last speck of make-up from her face. 'Besides, she might come in useful at some point,' she added. 'Anything's possible.'

Riding across the desert on the back of a golden horse with a band of Hajhi warriors, Zoë felt like someone out of the Arabian Nights. Even though she didn't know the route, she was close enough to the middle of the group that she could be guided if necessary and she was a good enough rider that the canter across the sand dunes didn't bother her.

Once Vaysha had accepted her identity, she had taken her back to join the rest of the Hajhi scouting party. Despite the patrol of the blue and silver soldiers the scouts were concealed on either side of the roadway and behind the rolling desert sand dunes. Their horses were crouched down behind a larger dune further back, as quiet as their masters as they too crouched down to the sand, their golden coats blending into the landscape.

With Vaysha to vouch for her, Zoë had been given the use of one of their spare horses when the scouts returned to camp. Although she knew that she could be safe just by finding the Door again she didn't like to mention it in front of Vaysha, doubting that Alex and Laura had let her in on their secret. But with the wind at her back Zoë didn't feel much like going home anyway and she grinned at Vaysha riding nearby when the other girl caught her eye.

The horses thundered across the desert as the sky lightened a little and, looking back, the massive bulk of Shattershard dwindled further and further into the distance. They were deep in the desert now. No roads or even tracks marked their way, the featureless dunes rolling up and down like waves around them, the echo of their hoof-beats the only sound. When the rhythm of the hooves finally slowed Zoë blinked and craned her neck to see past the lead riders to what lay ahead.

It was an army. Zoë knew that at first glance and, as the scouting party trotted closer, everything she saw only strengthened her conviction. The Hajhi tents might not have been laid out with military precision and the stockade of goats and shaggy cow creatures might not be much like the provisions of the British army, but the people standing around or sitting in front of the tents were armed for battle. When the scout group drew up and

Vaysha dismounted, Zoë imitated her and jumped down to the sandy ground, smiling when another scout took the reins of her horse for her and murmuring a thankyou.

'This way,' Vaysha said, taking Zoë's sleeve firmly. 'We go now to find Jhezra.'

Zoë nodded, although she realized that she wasn't exactly being offered a choice, and hoped that Jhezra remembered her. Now that she'd seen the Hajhi army she was feeling nervous about what the nomads might think of her being there.

Vaysha took her through the camp towards the embers of what had been a large fire, where a group of people not much older than Zoë were clustered together. The Hajhim gave Zoë curious glances as Vaysha led her past them and she smiled nervously in return, feeling out of place in her jeans and hooded top.

'Jhezra!' Vaysha called out suddenly, startling her. 'We were looking for you.'

'Here I am, then,' Jhezra said, turning away from the group she'd been talking to with a smile which froze on her face when she saw Zoë.

'You see why,' Vaysha said drily. 'I found this one outside the city, hiding from a Tetrarchate patrol.'

Jhezra looked at Zoë and then said slowly, 'You're lucky to be alive.'

'I know,' Zoë said, although she hadn't really and Jhezra's words sent a chill down her spine. This world was dangerous and she was only just beginning to realize how much.

'When I challenged her she said her name was Zoë and that she had friends who knew our people,' Vaysha continued to explain. 'She named Laura, which name I didn't recognize but now I recollect is Iskander's sister. Then Iskander, although she pronounced the name strangely. Then finally you, Jhezra, so I brought her to you.'

Jhezra looked at Zoë thoughtfully. Although they'd only met once before Zoë was beginning to get an idea of the Hajhi girl's personality. Jhezra was the kind of person who made quick decisions about people, either she accepted you or she didn't, and now she was considering what to do with Zoë.

'We must talk privately,' she said eventually and Vaysha laughed.

'I'll leave you to talk then,' she said. 'I have some reading to catch up on anyway.'

Zoë blinked at that but as Vaysha turned to leave she remembered to say, 'Thank you . . . um . . . for believing me.'

'Don't thank me yet,' Vaysha advised with a grimace of a smile. 'But good luck.' She nodded to Jhezra and left with a long easy stride to join the group that Jhezra had been talking to, leaving Jhezra and Zoë standing alone in the shadows at the edge of the camp.

They looked at each other. In this obvious war-camp with what must be hundreds of Hajhi warriors around and seeing Jhezra's scimitar and sickle-shaped dagger worn openly instead of hidden behind flapping robes, Zoë couldn't see Jhezra as the friendly nomad girl Laura had introduced her to and she suddenly remembered Morgan telling her 'Laura *lies*'. Wetting her lips she said out loud, 'The Hajhim are preparing to attack Shattershard and Alex and Laura are helping you.'

'That's true,' Jhezra said quietly. 'They have been helping us for a long time.'

'They let your people use their house and they . . . ' Zoë thought for a moment. 'They sell you things, things from—' She stopped abruptly.

'From Earth.'

Zoë stared. But at the same time she wasn't really all that surprised to hear Jhezra mention Earth. If Alex and

Laura were that deeply connected to the Hajhim it wasn't so strange that they'd have told their closest friend about themselves. Then she rethought that: Jhezra wasn't their *friend*, she was their contact.

'So you know about Earth,' Zoë said slowly, playing for time, and Jhezra smiled.

'Not much. Iskander brings us books sometimes. Vaysha buys texts on martial arts from him. But to the others he pretends to come from a far away country of our world. Only I know about his secret Door and not even where it is.' She paused and Zoë thought that with Vaysha's information about where Zoë had been found she could probably find it if she wanted.

'And you knew I come from the same place too,' she said.

'And Morgan. The magician girl who used to be a friend of Laura's and now lives in the city.' Jhezra nodded.

Zoë's mind caught on the way Jhezra had said that and, for the first time since Laura had explained about magicians to her, she wondered if Morgan really did have magic. Jhezra certainly seemed to assume it.

'I guess now I know you're preparing to attack the city I'm dangerous to you,' Zoë said, thinking quickly, but to her surprise Jhezra laughed.

'Everyone in Shattershard knows the Hajhim will attack,' she said. 'They have declared martial law within its walls and forbidden us to enter. The citizens have fled, leaving only the foolhardy, the city guard, and the Tetrarchate soldiers.' Her dark brown eyes were liquidly thoughtful as she gave Zoë a long look. 'What makes you dangerous is that you know Iskander and Laura are helping us.'

Zoë hesitated and then realized that even a moment's hesitation was too long.

'But Laura's my friend,' she said and it came out hollow. Jhezra's eyes darkened and Zoë shook her head quickly. 'No,' she said. 'That's not right. I don't know if she's my friend. But I won't tell on her. I mean . . . I don't know anything about this . . . I've only just seen your world. What's happening here isn't any of my business.'

'You mean that?' Jhezra said and Zoë nodded.

'I really do,' she said and it was true. 'I mean, in my own world I can't even tell my father about this. It's too incredible. In your world . . . ' She shook her head again. 'I don't even begin to understand what's happening and . . . ' she shrugged, 'and if Laura and Alex are on your side I guess I am too. It's not as if I even know anyone else here.'

'You know Morgan,' Jhezra said, but Zoë could tell it was just a reflex answer, the Hajhi girl was already convinced.

'I don't even speak to her at school,' she said and wondered how that would translate through her amulet until Jhezra laughed.

'Fair enough, then,' she said. 'You're on our side.'

And then to Zoë's surprise she reached out and clasped Zoë's hands. 'Welcome, friend,' she said.

'Thank you.' Zoë squeezed her hands back, feeling suddenly moved at Jhezra's whole-hearted acceptance of her, and tried to think of the best thing to say. 'Friends, then,' she said and meant it.

9

As a new day dawned over the desert Zoë sat on the edge of a sand dune and tried to re-adjust her attitude. A lot of things were becoming painfully clear to her now and she was trying to think them through. She was still carrying her small rucksack and she searched inside it for a while before coming up with a spiral-bound notebook and a pencil.

While the sun rose slowly and the Hajhi war-camp went about its business in what the light gradually made clear was an oasis of scrubby grasses and low bushes near a pool of surprisingly clear water, Zoë did mathematical sums on a new page of her notebook. She was trying to work out the time difference between Earth and the Tetrarchate world. Eventually she came to a conclusion and stood up, putting her notebook and pen back into her bag.

She walked down the side of the dune, slipping and sliding a little on the sand, and back into the camp and wasn't surprised when a Hajhi warrior came up to her side. He was a few years older than her and good looking, with flashing dark eyes and a long black plait of hair.

'I'm Tzandrian,' he said. 'A friend of Jhezra and Vaysha's. You're Jzohee?'

'That's right,' she said, then she frowned. 'Were you watching me?'

'Watching over you,' Tzandrian said. 'Jhezra asked me to.'

'OK then,' Zoë didn't waste time objecting, 'can you take me to find her?'

'Certainly.' Tzandrian gestured around the edge of the camp and Zoë fell into step with him as he started to walk.

As she'd already noticed, the camp was large and the number of warriors considerable. Most of them seemed to be armed with the curved sword and dagger combination she'd noticed so far but a few of them carried short bows as well or instead. There were horses everywhere, some corralled at the side of the camp but many just tied to posts in and around the strange round tents. Looking at them, Zoë noticed something she should have seen earlier.

'The saddles and stirrups,' she said, 'and the harnesses the horses wear. Is that a recent idea?'

Tzandrian didn't seem reluctant to talk and he shook his head with a quick smile of negation.

'It's been used for a while,' he said. 'Iskander showed us some improvements to the design.'

'Has he shown you a lot of improvements?' Zoë asked carefully, wondering what he would say.

'Not everyone agrees with his ideas,' Tzandrian told her. 'Not all of us are scholars like Vaysha.' He laughed and Zoë smiled back, not exactly sure of the joke, but remembering the warlike vision she'd first had of his friend.

'Does he sell you weapons?' she said, still thinking about Alex and remembering Morgan's comment about gun-running.

'He brings the things we use to make them,' Tzandrian told her and when Zoë looked mystified he pointed to an area set a little aside from the tents. There were stacked two different piles of items. The first group looked something like small catapults piled up next to each other. The second was a pile of drum-shaped barrels. Zoë had no idea what they were supposed to be.

She would have liked to ask Tzandrian to explain but as he led her past the things he had pointed out as weapons she felt nervous about seeming too curious. It had been a nasty moment when she'd thought Jhezra might consider her a spy and part of her was reluctant even to ask what things Alex had been selling to the Hajhim. It was alarming enough to realize that Morgan had been right. Instead she stayed silent until Tzandrian led her to a tent where Jhezra and Vaysha were sitting together sketching out something in the earthy sand of the ground.

'Zoë,' Jhezra said, looking up with a smile as they arrived and smoothing out the sketch on the ground with a gesture that made it look almost as if she was doing it to be polite. 'How are you?'

'I've been thinking a lot,' Zoë said, squatting down next to them on her heels the way the girls were sitting and seeing Tzandrian do the same beside her. 'And I think most of all that I should go home.'

'To the city?' Tzandrian said in surprise, looking at Jhezra rather than Zoë for an explanation.

'It's not safe . . . ' Vaysha began to say but Jhezra was only looking at Zoë.

'Very well,' she said. 'We have plans of our own but I think we can help you. Do you actually want to go inside Shattershard?' She gave Zoë a long look.

Zoë shook her head.

'If you could take me back to the place with the rocks where Vaysha found me,' she said. 'I'd appreciate it.'

'Just on the road?' Vaysha said but she was looking at Jhezra as well now.

'We can do that,' Jhezra said, looking at each of them in turn before stopping with Zoë. 'What will you do after that?' she asked.

'I honestly don't know,' Zoë admitted and Jhezra shrugged fluidly before turning the motion into a stretch and standing up again.

'It doesn't matter,' she said. 'But Vaysha has a point. Neither Shattershard or the desert are likely to be very safe for a while. You might want to bear that in mind.'

Although the sun was already visible in the sky, the central caldera of the mountain of Shattershard was too overshadowed by the high rock walls to catch the light of dawn. Even the city palace high up on the mountainside was cold and dark despite the clear blue sky above and Morgan, leaving by a side entrance, shivered a little as she came out into the steep street.

Although Kal had offered to send her back to the magical guild-house by carriage she'd told him she preferred to walk. It gave her some time to think. Ciren and Charm would be waiting at the guild-house and they'd want to talk to her about their plans. Ever since they'd explained to her about the existence of the Collegiate they'd made it clear they considered themselves somehow responsible for her and that they'd like her to trust them. To a certain extent she was willing to, since there had been no repetition of the dizzy spell she'd had in Charm's presence before. But there were things she didn't feel able to tell them and they were the same things she was concealing from Kal.

Morgan sighed, gathering her long black cloak up around herself as she went down an abrupt flight of steps that acted as a short cut from the street she was on to a lower one curving around the mountainside. All she'd really wanted was to spend time in Shattershard and to do magic. When she'd found out that Laura and Alex had bigger plans she'd broken away from them, disliking Alex's condescension and Laura's proprietorial attitude towards Shattershard. But now she wished she'd stayed around for long enough to find out what exactly their plan really was. She knew they were supplying the Hajhim with military advantages and weapons as well as acting as spies for their raiding parties and ambushes on the caravans. But she didn't doubt that there was an overall purpose to it and that the Harrells had some extra scheme to attack the city.

Now she was seeing Kal, she finally had a good reason to give away Laura and Alex's secret, especially since they seemed to be ignoring the laws of the city, but she still felt uncomfortable about breaking her promise to them. At least Kal, although he kept trying to find out what she was hiding, hadn't guessed yet what she knew. But Ciren and Charm had. They were certain she knew who was responsible for the Hajhim's military successes and they'd asked her more or less straight out to tell them.

Cutting across another street along an arched stone bridge and down a little flight of stairs, Morgan bit her lips. Nothing seemed to be straightforward now and every option seemed like a betrayal. This was exactly the kind of thing she'd been trying to get away from when she'd started coming through the Door Between Worlds, the difficulty of knowing where your loyalties should lie.

Reaching the double doors of the guild-house she

opened the smaller door inset into the side of one of them with her key and went inside. Although a new day was beginning outside there was no sign of stirring inside the building as she went up the stairs and along the corridors to her room. When she got there she didn't bother reaching for the other key she carried but simply turned the handle and walked in.

'Hello, twins,' she said.

'Hello, Morgan.' Ciren looked up from his position at the table where a board of game pieces had been laid out.

'Morgan, hello,' Charm echoed from her place across from him. 'We were waiting for you.'

Morgan undid the tie of her cloak and hung it up on a hook on the back of the door before getting a drink of water from the dolphin-shaped tap at the corner of the room. When she came back to the table she said, 'You know this is *my* room.'

'For all the time you spend in it,' Ciren agreed. 'We were worried about you.'

'God!' Morgan frowned at them, not sure how annoyed she really was but wanting to get through to them. 'Since when is my life your business?'

'Since you joined the Collegiate,' Charm said, looking up at her. 'This world is dangerous, Morgan.'

'And Shattershard more than most places,' Ciren continued, picking up the chain of conversation. 'And at the Archon's side most dangerous of all.'

Morgan sat down, still holding her glass of water, and looked across at the twins. In the last few days her life had changed out of all recognition. Earth and Weybridge seemed a million lifetimes away. She suddenly realized why it was that she wasn't annoyed with the Collegiate twins. It was because in all the world, in all both worlds, they were the only people who tried to understand her without assuming automatically that they did.

'Is it really that dangerous?' she asked now. 'I feel . . . not really that it's my home but . . . it's a place I'm more connected to than my own world.' She paused. 'Also, there's Kal.' She couldn't help the blush that rose then but when neither Ciren or Charm reacted to it, it gradually faded again.

'I think it will be that dangerous,' Charm said. 'We told you we were travelling agents, making notes on the places we visit for other Collegiate members to study. In situations like this we'd generally leave and not come back until the region had settled down again.'

'But now we have to consider your wishes too,' Ciren added. 'You're new to the Collegiate and have fewer resources.' He looked at Morgan, purple-black eyes searching her face, before adding: 'And there are the others you're protecting. The other travellers from your world. If we can we must try to tell them about the Collegiate and its rules. And help them escape from here if they agree to abide by them.'

When Jhezra left Zoë at the rocky outcrop half a mile outside the city, Vaysha and Tzandrian had been confused. But the rest of their band, ten Hajhi warriors in all, hadn't questioned it. As far as they were concerned, the heads of the war council had told them to obey Jhezra and Zoë's strange choice of destination was just part of the Plan.

The Plan had been carefully designed to adapt to the new situation in Shattershard and once Zoë had been taken care of, Jhezra was ready to move on to the first stage. But meeting the Earth girl had made her thoughtful and while the warriors rested in the shade of the rocks, quietly going over their parts in what was to come next, Jhezra stood looking into the desert and wondered.

She hadn't intended to make a gesture of friendship

towards Zoë. When Vaysha had returned from scouting with the red-headed girl in tow her heart had sunk, seeing Zoë as a problem to be factored in. But when they had talked, she'd been surprised to find herself thinking of Zoë as a person like herself, in a way that she hadn't really ever thought of Iskander. In fact even the way that Zoë called Iskander 'Alex' and plainly thought of him as the brother of her friend had strengthened the feeling of familiarity. When she had met Iskander and Laura, they'd been secretive about their origins and when Iskander had finally told her the truth she'd been awed by his tales of travelling between worlds. Even when they'd become lovers she still felt that awe for him and for his secretive spy of a sister. Morgan she'd been confused by, finding the black-mage disconcerting and impossible to understand. But Zoë was like a friend. Like Vaysha or Tzandrian. A person with feelings and fears that were real to Jhezra to an extent she hadn't expected.

A shadow fell across her and she looked up to see Tzandrian looking down at her.

'Stare at the sand too long and you'll be blown away on the wind,' he said, repeating the substance of a cautionary tale told to children. 'What next, O great leader?'

'The city is next,' Jhezra said, putting her strange thoughts away from her. 'And by a road we won't much enjoy.'

Vaysha, coming to join them, caught her words and grimaced.

'Sewers,' she said, rolling her eyes. 'Well, since the Tetrarchate thinks of us like their filth anyway . . . '

'Whatever road brings us to victory is fine by me,' Tzandrian said, shrugging.

'And it won't become sweeter for us delaying,' Jhezra agreed. 'Come then.' She glanced towards the rest of the war-band and added louder, 'Two will string the horses together and take them back to the camp. The rest go on to the city with me.'

The subject of Alex and Laura had come up again and Morgan studied the twins, knowing already how hard it was to read them. Although Charm was mostly serious around her and Ciren the more friendly of the two she guessed that their behaviour might change when they were alone. Part of Charm's chariness might well come from the fact that she had read Morgan's mind before and hadn't exactly promised not to again.

Morgan wanted to believe that Ciren and Charm were being honest with her. If they truly did want to help world-travellers, then telling them about Alex and Laura wouldn't seem such a betrayal. But although she'd become more used to the twins, she knew how powerful they were and she didn't doubt that they could be dangerous enemies.

'You told me about the rules before,' she said at last. 'But not all together. Is there a list or something? Of what they are and how they work?'

'There are many,' Ciren said immediately. 'And they don't all agree. The Collegiate is . . . a complicated thing to explain. To really understand it you'd have to see the Great Library. The place where we meet and where the books we write and collect are kept.'

Morgan frowned and Charm leaned forward a little.

'It's true,' she said softly. 'The Collegiate is a . . . ' she paused, obviously searching for the right words, 'a *large* thing to understand. And our rules aren't exactly rules, or laws, or guidelines but . . . '

'Articles of faith,' Ciren finished. 'So we can't exactly list them for you completely but we can explain them some more.'

'OK.' Morgan nodded. Then she hesitated. 'Can I write this down?'

Ciren laughed out loud and although Charm didn't smile she bent her head forward over the table so her shoulder-length hair fell briefly forward to conceal the front of her face in a gesture that seemed strangely like a smile.

'Of course,' Ciren said, still laughing, waving Morgan to her desk where her notebooks and pens were laid out. 'Of course you must write it down. But, Morgan, now you see why some things are hard for us to understand. Collegiate members all keep books and the Collegiate is . . . '

'A very large thing to understand.' Morgan laughed too, getting it at last. She got a thick leather-bound book with blank pages and a pen from the desk and brought them back to the table, opening the book at the first double blank page. 'OK, and this Great Library must have a lot of books in it.'

'Many and a hundred times many,' Charm said.

'Written in different languages,' Ciren added. 'Fiction and fact. Speculation and story. Mysteries and musings. An eternity of books.'

'Where is it?' Morgan asked and Ciren smiled.

'That's the beginning of what we have to tell you,' Charm said. 'Most Collegiate members memorize a litany of Doors. Of the travels you must take across worlds and between them to bring you back to a safe place.'

'A Safe Place,' Morgan said, her hand automatically writing as she listened to the twins, and capitalizing the words on the page.

'The Library is one,' Ciren told her. 'At least for the most part, although it has its own dangers. And also there are worlds more civilized than others. Even a few where world-travellers are known of and accepted.'

'If there are those, we've yet to visit them,' Charm said with a dry edge to her words. 'Such places are legend.'

'No, not legend.' Ciren contradicted his twin for the first time and Morgan looked up, arrested. 'The Great Library after all is one such world and Caravaggion of Mandarel writes that there may be others: riddled with Doors and populated only by people who know of them and use them.'

'I'd like to see a place like that,' Morgan said and Charm turned to her.

'You can see the Great Library,' she said. 'At least we can share with you a litany of Doors that will take you there. There's a Door to the Library from this very world. From the capital city.'

'It's the one we used to come here,' Ciren explained. His pale pointed face turned to glance at its mirror in his twin's eyes for a moment before he looked back at Morgan with an air of importance about him. 'You know something of Charm's power already. Mine is to sense magic and by extension the presence of Doors. That's how we knew there would be world-travellers in this city. Because I sensed the presence of Doors.'

'More than one?' Morgan said, staggered, and Charm nodded.

'That seemed strange to me too but Ciren insists that it is not so unusual. Apparently Caravaggion of Mandarel is an authority on the subject.'

Ciren laughed and Morgan did too. She didn't know how but she knew that Charm had made a joke because she wanted them to laugh and although the pale-haired girl didn't so much as smile Morgan was getting used to that and she grinned at Charm before turning serious again.

'But if there's more than one Door, then where?'

'There's one outside the city,' Charm said. 'Which

we've waited to investigate because of the trouble with the Hajhim. And another under the city which so far we haven't been able to find.'

Morgan hesitated for only a second.

'Mine is the one in the desert,' she said. 'My world is called Earth.' She glanced down at her translation amulet suddenly. 'I don't know how well that translates,' she added.

'As a name,' Ciren said. '*Urth*. And also as a noun, a word for a thing that exists.' He pointed at the floor. 'Ground. But with the meaning of soil, the stuff of living things.'

'That's right,' Morgan nodded. 'All of that.' She thought for a moment. 'But how come you couldn't find the other Door?'

'There is a warren of tunnels under the city,' Ciren explained. 'Storage rooms and cellars, natural caves in the mountain and tunnels carved by magic for water to run through, the reservoir and sewer system of the city. Somewhere in all of that I sense a Door. But with the twists and turns of the tunnels we haven't found it yet.'

'Although we look for it every day,' Charm added. 'Do you want to come with us today when we look?'

'Of course,' Morgan said, surprising herself with her immediate acceptance. 'And also I want you to tell me more about the Collegiate and about the rules for acceptance.'

'And will you tell us the names of the other world-travellers then?' Ciren asked. 'Do you understand yet that as Collegiate members it is our duty to find them and educate them about what we know?'

Morgan looked at the twins.

'I think I almost do,' she said softly. 'But I did promise . . . ' She looked pleadingly at Ciren. 'If you could give me just a little more time?'

*   *   *

The gate guards of Shattershard slumped a bit at their posts. With the Tetrarchate soldiers assiduously checking and rechecking the passes of everyone who approached the gate, there was little for them to do. Despite the fact that it was mid-morning, usually the busiest part of the day as caravans that had camped the night before in the desert hastened into Shattershard for the day's trading, there were few people on the road. For the past few days the Hajhim had been absent too. Not even the pedlar children who usually stationed themselves outside the gates, selling strings of cheap beads and roughly dyed cotton, had been seen coming out of the desert.

Up above on the gate towers the guards likewise yawned. Tetrarchate soldiers still manned the tower heights, keeping a close watch on the sand where for miles there was no sign of warriors or armies, while the Shattershard guards watched the blue sky and drank deeply from the water skins they swapped about, refilling them from the reservoirs built into the guard towers.

But there was one place left unwatched and unguarded. As the system of pipes funnelled water through the rock of the mountain city and spilled it into kitchens and shower rooms, sluicing the waste-water that returned through the channels of the toilet shafts and the middens, it ended its journey at the base of the mountain to fertilize the soil-pits there. Mixed with the fertilizing sewage, the sand at the base of the rock became crumbled and earthy and could be used as soil for the gardens up in the towers of Shattershard. Now and again men would brave the stench of the pits to cart barrels of earthy waste back up to the city again, but today the muddy pits were abandoned.

The Hajhim had turned their sand robes inside out to show the grey-dyed sides they had prepared. Moving slowly across the rocks that ringed the soil-pits, they kept careful watch on the heights above. There were battlements there and towers, but the guards were watching the desert, not the mountain, and with any luck no one would see them as they made their way through the filth.

'There,' Jhezra said softly, raising her hand carefully to point up the rocky mountainside. The black rock was wet with slime and mould, and water trickled down constantly from a series of spouts, sometimes sluicing forth with a sudden gush into the pit, but always dripping and sliding down the craggy mountain.

'I see it,' Vaysha said at her side and turned back to pass the word along the line.

'I'll go first,' Jhezra said, wrapping the climbing rope tightly around her waist. They had practised for this in the desert crags and when she let the rest of the length of the rope drop to the rock beside her, Tzandrian was there to mind it for her, holding it carefully to let out slack as she began to climb.

The place she was aiming for was a fissure in the rock, the channels carved by magic spilling out through a natural cave with a crumbling entrance. Jhezra had followed this route twice before, once on her own, once with Tzandrian, and confirmed what she had suspected. This route taken from the city by all the waste and filth of Shattershard could be climbed in the other direction by Hajhim to enact the first stage of the Plan she and Iskander had thought up.

She climbed with care, flattening herself to the rock and searching for hand-holds and foot-holds along the fetid crevices of the mountain and on the dripping water-spouts. Several times she was caught in a gush of waste from above and bent her head away from the filth as it cascaded past her. The two times she had done this before she had thrown up her stomach's contents into the rest of the waste and now, although she hadn't eaten that day, she retched spasmodically when she finally made the lip of the cave and crawled up into its mouth.

'The rope is fast,' she whispered down to the others below and saw Tzandrian brace himself as Vaysha took hold of the rope's length and began to haul herself up.

Vaysha arrived at the cave more quickly with the rope to help her than Jhezra had on her own but her face was set in a grimace as she pulled herself over and stepped away from the rope. Below, the next warrior began to climb and Jhezra looked up from watching the rope to glance at her friend.

'Are you well?' she asked quietly and Vaysha nodded, then bent over suddenly to hack up her first meal by the side of the cave.

'I'm well,' she said, standing and wiping the back of her arm across her mouth, avoiding the touch of her own clothing. 'But you were right to warn us to fast before this. I feel as if I will never be clean again.'

'It will get worse before it gets better,' Jhezra warned. 'But higher up there are places of clean water where we can wash off the worst of it.'

'I'm well,' Vaysha repeated. 'Shall I watch the rope?'

Tzandrian was the last to arrive at the cave and by then Jhezra had shown the other five the path upwards into one of the larger channels that had broken through into the cave. Once Tzandrian and Vaysha had joined them she took the head of the line, carrying a shielded lantern to light the way through the blackness. The channel was slippery and the waste lay clogged on its floor. Several times more she had to climb the rocky side of higher chutes with the rope tied to her waist, but as the others got used to the technique they took turns, holding lanterns to show each other the way, playing the light up and down the channels and fissures in the rock.

When they finally reached a level place and a chamber where the water and waste was guided in open tanks and filtered down to the chutes below, Jhezra called a halt for a while. Like the others she washed herself in some of the cleaner water, full of floating kitchen waste rather than sewage, and sat on a stone cistern for a rest.

'This is a hell of a place,' Vaysha said, wringing out her headcloth emphatically. 'Do the city people even know it's here?'

'I've not once seen a person this far below,' Jhezra told her. 'But the sewage system goes on for miles and miles of tunnels under the city, and on some of the higher levels there are signs that people go there to make repairs.' She shrugged. 'I think perhaps we are the first to be here since these tunnels were made.'

'Otherwise the city folk might guess about the gap in their defences,' Tzandrian said grimly and other warriors hearing him nodded, encouraged by the thought.

'You couldn't bring an army this way,' Vaysha said quietly. 'But this work doesn't need one.' She glanced at Jhezra. 'This was a cunning plan.'

'Iskander deserves the credit for the whole of it,' Jhezra reminded her and Vaysha shrugged.

'Iskander isn't getting his pretty clothes all messed up by it,' she said.

While Jhezra and her band were finding a grim humour in their unpleasant task, there were others exploring the same network of corridors. In what had become a familiar routine, Charm unravelled a long thread of twine to mark their path as Ciren concentrated on the maze of magic corridors, planning their route in his head. But today a third person accompanied them, one hand holding the chain of a witch-light that glowed faintly from the soft whisper of magic in its owner's mind. Morgan walked between the twins as they explored the passages of the under-city, keeping her voice as low as theirs as they talked to prevent the echoes from overwhelming them.

They were continuing from a place the twins had marked as the furthest extent of their explorations so far, an area beneath the Archon's palace, and Morgan was awed by the sheer number of the tunnels carved into the black rock.

'What's all of this for?' she said, not for the first time, as they emerged into another empty chamber with a choice of more than one exit. Archways led in three directions and staircases went up and down to a fourth and fifth while a chute guided water down an unpleasant sixth option. 'It seems crazed.'

'Some of this might have been mining tunnels originally,' Ciren speculated. 'And there's the water channels and chambers, of course. And a lot of the tunnels open in and out of natural caves in the rock.'

'But all the same,' Morgan said, as they took the staircase downwards, Charm letting out the twine behind them. 'It's . . . eerie.'

'I've seen stranger things than this,' Charm told her quietly. 'But I've wondered if maybe the tunnels were built by someone else with Ciren's power searching for a Door they could sense inside the rock.'

'Is that possible?' Morgan asked in wonder. 'A Door that opened inside a *mountain*?'

'I don't know,' Ciren said. 'I've heard of Doors in the air and Doors under the earth but . . . ' His voice trailed away. 'The stories sounded like myths. I've never known anyone who'd found one.'

'Well, you wouldn't have, would you, twin?' Charm's voice was calm behind them as she pointed out: 'Because anyone who'd found one would have learnt about it the hard way, falling from a height or suffocating underground.'

'That's a nasty thought.' Morgan shuddered and she saw Ciren nod ahead of her.

'If it was meant to be reassuring it certainly failed,' he said. 'There are enough dangers for the unwary world-traveller without inventing more.'

Morgan thought about that for a while as the boy-twin led them on through the tunnels. She wondered what sort of dangers he meant and her mind began an unpleasant list of them. Not only could there be local people who were hostile to travellers, there must also be danger from wild animals in jungles or forests and perhaps the risk of thirst or starvation if a Door opened in the middle of a desert or wasteland. Magic also might be a problem. She knew that her own magic and the amulets and talismans sold in the city didn't work back on Earth. What if she stepped through a Door into another world where they didn't function? Without them she'd have been helpless in Shattershard.

She opened her mouth to ask Ciren or Charm for an explanation of that but before she could speak Charm said out loud, 'Do you hear that noise?'

They all came to a halt and listened, Morgan craning her head to hear something and Ciren stilling into what she was coming to recognize as his trance for sensing magical signatures.

'All I hear is water,' Morgan whispered after a few minutes.

Throughout their journey the sound of water had been a constant companion, trickling or gushing through the pipes and cisterns that passed through and around the tunnels.

'The water noise is changed here,' Charm said. 'It's

louder and more regular. Like a thrumming thundering noise instead of a cascading sound.'

Morgan frowned, trying to hear the change, and Ciren said thoughtfully, 'The Door's beneath us still and to the left of our bearing. I think that's the direction the water comes from as well.'

'Then let's continue,' Charm said instantly.

'But with care,' Ciren answered and Morgan lifted the witch-light high to light their way.

It wasn't long before they discovered the source of the change in the sound of the water. The slope they were descending came to an abrupt halt that would have been a shock if Ciren hadn't called softly to warn them of it, spilling the three of them out on to a ledge overlooking a large natural cavern filled deep with water. The witch-light reflected off crystalline rocks in the walls and ceiling and across the choppy surface of the pool. Two great columns of rock came down into the pool and these were the source of the thundering rush of noise that Charm had first identified. From one, underneath where it sank into the water, came bubbles rising to the surface in foaming waves. From the base of the other was a swirling current like a plughole in reverse as the water appeared to be sucked into the base of the column.

'What is it?' Morgan called out, having to strain to be heard over the noise of the water.

'Ancient magic,' Charm told her. 'It must be part of the water system.'

'Whatever its purpose it has ended our search,' Ciren told them. 'I can sense the Door clearly now.' He pointed into the pool below with a fatalistic shrug. 'It's right at the bottom of that.'

10

When Jhezra left her at the rocks, Zoë hadn't hesitated to use the Door to get back to her world. The wood on the other side was cold and grey with the smell of autumn evening and she realized how long she'd been gone with alarm, hurrying back through the trees and out on to the road. Outside Laura's house she stopped for only a second. Laura wouldn't be back yet, she was sure. She and Alex must still be in Shattershard, making their plans to take over the city and she wondered how they managed to sneak their travels past their parents.

At the thought of Laura's mother she started walking again, just in case Mrs Harrell could see her standing outside the house, thinking that Alex and Laura might run rings around their parents but she wouldn't like to try. There was a bus stop at the bottom of Bicken Hill and she waited for twenty minutes before a bus going to the other side of town arrived.

By the time she got home Zoë knew she was in trouble

and when she let herself into the house her dad was standing in the living room looking grim.

'I'm sorry,' she said immediately. 'I went to see Laura, I lost track of time. Sorry.'

'Doesn't Laura have a phone?' he asked and Zoë winced.

'Um, I didn't think to ask,' she said. 'When I realized it was late I just came straight home. Um . . . sorry.'

Her dad looked at her and then he frowned.

'This isn't like you, Zozo,' he said. 'What's up?'

'Nothing,' Zoë said quickly. 'Nothing, not really.' She hesitated and then said, to herself as much as to him, 'I'm not going back there, that's all.'

'Oh.' Her dad suddenly stopped looking angry and stretched out a comforting hand. 'Did you have an argument with Laura, is that it?'

'Sort of.' Zoë swallowed uncomfortably. 'She's . . . she's not who she seems to be.'

She didn't know what else to say and after a moment her dad squeezed her shoulder, while she looked down at the pale brown carpet.

'OK then,' he said. 'These things happen. Court martial over, soldier, charges dismissed and don't do it again. Let's send out for some pizza, shall we?'

It was hard even to nod, Zoë felt so guilty for lying to him. But she didn't intend to go back and she ate pizza and watched TV with him, forcing herself to come back to normal and trying to forget about Shattershard. What she told him had been true. Her last encounter with the other world had been dangerous enough to scare her and she had decided on the journey home that it would be stupid to risk going back there, at least for a little while. Maybe when Laura and Alex and Jhezra had won their war against the city, as Jhezra seemed confident they would, she could go back then. But Zoë couldn't help thinking that the war might cause more trouble than the Harrells had intended and wondered if perhaps Laura and Alex might just disappear some day and that would be the last she ever heard of Shattershard.

That reminded her of Morgan's mother and she wondered uneasily if Morgan had come back from the city yet. If she'd really disappeared it might be on the local news but Zoë didn't want to try to find out. All the same she found it hard to stop thinking about it. Morgan had told her that Laura and Alex were gun-runners, Morgan had told her that Laura lied; Morgan the Goth girl that Zoë had consciously avoided at school, who dressed in the black that meant magic in Shattershard.

'What's on your mind, soldier?' her dad asked gently and Zoë curled up next to him on the sofa and said:

'A girl at school, called Morgan.' She added reluctantly, 'I called her house on . . . on Monday, I think it was, and her mother said she hadn't come home.'

'Oh.' Her dad frowned. 'Is she a good friend of yours?'

'I don't know her at all really,' Zoë admitted. 'I thought she was kind of a weirdo, you see. But . . . I don't know. There was just something I wanted to ask her . . . But it was freaky her mum saying she hadn't been home. She sounded . . . I don't know . . . '

'Sounds as if this girl might be in some kind of trouble,' Zoë's dad said and then asked, 'Do you think I should call Morgan's mother?'

'No!' Zoë shook her head. 'I mean . . . what could you say? I don't even know her. It just . . . scared me a bit. That's all.'

Her dad nodded, putting a comforting arm around her and Zoë hugged him back, trying to concentrate on who she was here in the real world.

But when she went to bed that night she had bad

dreams. She dreamt about riding through the desert, her muscles aching as she forced the horse onwards and away from blue and silver soldiers she knew were out there in the dark behind her. Then she was scrabbling against the rock to reach the Door she knew was there but it was too dark to see and she couldn't find it. She woke more than once and each time it took her ages to get back to sleep; each time she ended up thinking about Morgan, and her eyes ached when she finally fell asleep again just as the sky was greying to dawn.

The last time she dreamt she was standing in the desert with Jhezra in the darkness of the war-camp.

'It's dangerous here,' Jhezra said. *'Whose side are you on?'*

'I'm Laura's friend,' Zoë said in her dream.

Then Jhezra turned into Morgan and it was the palace court that surrounded them. Morgan's eyes, green like Laura's but darkened by her black eyeliner, stared into hers.

'Laura lies,' she whispered.

Zoë was tired all through the next morning. Her dad had left for work early and when she got up there was a note waiting for her on the breakfast table, propped up on the milk jug, reading: 'Have a good day, soldier. See you at 1900. Love, Major Dad.' She smiled at it and poured herself some cereal, determined to spend the day being as normal as possible.

She went out to the rec ground after breakfast and found some of the younger kids playing football out there. Sitting on the swings at the other end, Zoë watched them for a while. Army brats moved around a lot but lots of them made the time they spent in any one place count. Even though you knew that friends would move away sooner or later, or you would, most of the kids banded together to hang out or play games. Zoë had had some friends on other bases from the kids there and although she'd had less time with them than kids at school, they'd tended to be better friends. Army brats understood the importance of friendship. Maybe someone like Laura who'd lived in the same place all her life took it for granted.

Swinging idly back and forth it took a while to notice that the man walking round the side of the rec ground towards the houses was her dad. She jumped up in surprise, wondering what he was doing back so early, and ran to meet him as he arrived at the door.

'Where did you spring from?' he asked, turning as she came through the gate, his hand still turning the handle.

'I was on the rec ground,' Zoë said, following him inside. 'How come you're back so soon, Major Dad?'

He grinned at her, ruffling her hair, but then he looked serious.

'I'm sorry about this, Zozo,' he said. 'But it seems I have to go away again for a couple of days . . . '

'Dad! No!' Zoë cut him off. 'You were gone last weekend! It's not *fair*.'

'I know.' He frowned but he was shaking his head. 'But it can't be helped. You'll just have to soldier on without me for a couple of days.'

Zoë's heart sank. Without her dad around to help her be normal, she felt as if Shattershard would suck her into its world. It had been hard enough not to think about it just this morning and she didn't know if she could manage it for days.

'Do you really have to go?' she pleaded, knowing it was useless.

'I really do,' he said, hugging her. 'Come on, little soldier, shape up. You'll be fine for a couple of days. Mrs Siefer said she'll keep an eye on you and she invited you to go round and eat with them if you want to. You'll be OK.'

'Yeah.' There was no point making him feel bad. 'But I don't need to go and eat with the Siefers. I'll be OK here.' She summoned a grin. 'Probably have some wild parties and invite drug-dealers round.'

'You do that, Zozo.' Her dad dropped a kiss on top of her head. 'I'm going to pack a bag and then I'm out of here. I'll see you about lunch time on Friday, OK?'

'Orders received and understood, sir.' Zoë saluted. 'I'll hold the fort while you're gone.'

He left not long afterwards and this time Zoë didn't go out. She'd hugged him one last time before he left the house and tried not to feel as if she was saying goodbye to him forever. She felt as if her dad was slipping further and further away from her and that she had no idea how to hold on to him. Lying on her bed in her room she remembered asking Laura if the world on the other side of the Door was like Narnia. Alex had told her it was, but in truth it hadn't been anything like the story books. Shattershard wasn't a fantasy, it was horribly real. However, she remembered how the Narnia children had always had parents who weren't really around very much and wondered if there was something about kids who went into other worlds that meant they were less connected to other people than most. Maybe you found a Door into another world because you weren't properly fixed in this one.

It didn't do any good to dwell on it, she told herself, because she wasn't going into Shattershard again. But all through that day she found herself looking at her pieces of evidence, the things she had kept to prove Shattershard was real: the translation amulet Laura had given her and the box full of desert sand in her desk drawer; also the calculations she had scrawled in her notebook while sitting on the side of the sand dune in the desert.

That night she found herself dialling Morgan's number but she hung-up before the phone could ring. She tried twice more and the third time someone snatched up the phone before she'd even finished dialling and she realized that she'd accidentally let it connect.

'Who's there?' a man's voice demanded and then added, 'If that's you, Morgan, you can forget it! She ain't having you back in the house.' Then he hung up and Zoë let the receiver clatter back on to the handset, feeling shaky and her hands suddenly damp with sweat.

Morgan wasn't home and maybe Laura and Alex weren't either. She didn't want to call the Harrells' house and she doubted they would answer if she did. Zoë went to bed before it was late, just wanting to sleep and forget about it all. That night her dreams were lonely. She sat on the swings of the rec ground and all the friends she had made at her past schools stood on the other side of the fence ignoring her.

Zoë went to the Door for the last time on Thursday night. She hadn't meant to but as the day wore on she found herself in her room, sorting through her wardrobe for an army kitbag she'd sometimes used as a school bag. It started out as an intellectual exercise: if she was going back, what should she take with her? But when she let herself out of the house and locked the door behind her she knew she was going to go through the Door Between Worlds.

She was wearing the present her dad had brought her from Germany: the creamy-leather army coat with the folded-over collar. Over her shoulder she carried a scruffy white kitbag with S. T. Kaul printed near the drawstring. The things she'd decided to bring with her were very basic. In one pocket she had a Swiss army pocket knife and a Zippo lighter and in her bag she had a bottle of water and her dad's binoculars as well as a couple of home-made sandwiches.

'I'm prepared,' she told herself as she left the base. 'Like a scout. Dob dob dob.'

The bus across town didn't seem to take so long this time and she didn't stop at the Harrells' house when she took the nature track into the Weywode Forest. Noticing everything on her journey as if it were for the first time, she wondered about the name of the wood and about Weybridge itself. What if in ancient times people had known about the Door? But it was difficult to concentrate. She still couldn't believe that she was doing this and when she arrived at the clearing in the Weywode Forest she stood staring at the impossible blackness of the Door beneath the shadows of the trees.

She'd timed it carefully this time. It was evening on Earth and the musty brown smell of autumn leaves was mixed with the cold snap of winter in the air. By her calculations that meant it was morning in the desert. The city gate would be open and she could go through into Shattershard and find Laura. What she didn't know was what she would do then.

'Well, look at you. All tooled up and ready for action,' a voice sneered behind her and Zoë jumped.

It was Morgan. She stood in the wooded clearing dressed in her usual black but she didn't look anything like the shy Goth Zoë knew from school. Her long black hair was piled up on her head and secured with a silver barrette instead of hanging in a tangled curtain in front of her face and her green eyes were dark and unreadable as she stared at Zoë.

'Suiting up for the final battle?' Morgan continued. 'Or just planning to mix it up on your own account?'

'It's not like that!' Zoë said quickly and she stared back at Morgan, wondering what she could say. 'It's . . . it's just not, OK? I didn't mean to come here.'

'But here you are,' Morgan pointed out.

It was strange. The black-haired girl didn't sound anything like herself. Although she was obviously hostile she didn't seem nervous or even especially angry, just challenging. She seemed oddly confident and that was enough to make up Zoë's mind.

'Look, I'm sorry I didn't listen to you before,' she said. 'When you told me about Laura.'

'Oh?' Morgan's catlike eyes narrowed and Zoë wondered why she'd never noticed that Morgan was actually attractive. Suddenly thinking of Jhezra she found herself wondering if Morgan, like Alex, had a lover in the desert world.

'It's not because of Laura I'm going back,' she said. 'I mean . . . I want to talk to her but . . . it's not because of that . . . ' She looked helplessly around the clearing and then back at Morgan. 'I just . . . I need to know what's going to happen. Another world . . . it's too incredible for me to just walk away from.'

Her eyes pleaded with Morgan to understand and the other girl glanced down at the ground, for a moment looking more like the old Morgan, then she raised her head to look at Zoë again. Her expression was curious, as if she was really seeing her for the first time.

'That's just how I feel,' she admitted eventually. 'That's why I'm going back.' She shrugged a shoulder, showing Zoë the black haversack she was carrying, and then looked cold again. 'For good this time.'

'Forever?' Zoë stared. 'How can you?'

'As it turns out, very easily,' Morgan told her, moving

to join her in front of the Door. She glanced across at Zoë. 'Look,' she said. 'I have to go. But . . . if you're really certain you want to do this there's some stuff you should know.' She hesitated. 'Come on, if you're coming,' she said and walked towards the Door.

'Wait!'

Zoë reached out abortively as Morgan moved past her and stepped, without a moment's hesitation, through the Door. The inky blackness of the space between worlds swallowed her instantly and she was gone. Zoë looked wildly around the clearing, feeling the chill of the evening around her, and then back at the Door. There was no time left to think. Clutching the string of her kitbag she hurried after Morgan and through the Door.

On the other side she stumbled into brightness and had to stagger to recover her balance on the rough surface of the rocks. A new day was dawning over the desert and ahead of her Morgan was stepping on to the beaten track of the road. Hurrying to catch up, Zoë called after her, and the black figure turned and waited on the path ahead.

Morgan and Zoë walked up the slowly climbing road to Shattershard as the sun coloured the expanse of sand all around them with glimmering gold. The sky was clear and still and their shadows stretched out ahead of them on the road. Morgan looked at the stark black shapes, her own thin and elongated into a spectral creature with attenuated fingers and Zoë's flapping coat giving her wings and a great crest of a collar crowned with wild tendrils of curly hair.

Morgan hadn't expected to find anyone at the Door although she'd mentally braced for the possibility that Laura or Alex might be around. Zoë had surprised her in more ways than one and she wasn't really sure what to say to the other girl. Even though she knew Zoë had despised her in Weybridge, that didn't really seem important now that she thought of herself as a member of the Collegiate.

'Are you really leaving for good?' Zoë asked in a quiet voice and Morgan bit her lip.

'Yeah,' she said softly. 'Back in Weybridge I don't . . . Stuff with my mum's kind of fucked up. I only went back today to collect some things. I don't have any reason to go back now.'

'Do you think Alex and Laura are planning the same thing?'

'I have no idea.' Morgan shook her head vehemently. 'And I'd appreciate you not telling them about me.' She glanced across at Zoë and saw the other girl nod quickly and wondered if she believed her. 'You know I'm not friends with them,' she said.

'I know,' Zoë agreed. 'I don't know if I'm really friends with them but . . . ' She spread her hands. 'I have to see them,' she finished.

Morgan wasn't sure what to say about that and they walked on in silence for a while. Going up the road to Shattershard was eerie knowing that there were Tetrarchate soldiers watching them from every battlement and tower-height. The great rock arch of the city gates loomed ahead and Morgan raised her chin as she saw the city guards and blue and silver troops waiting for them. At her side she felt Zoë inhale sharply as two soldiers stepped to block their way.

'Passes, ladies,' one of them said firmly and Morgan reached into her bag pulling out her Shattershard papers.

'Here,' she said, watching while the guards checked them and unable to help herself grinning when they came to the most recent confirmation of her right to enter the city signed with the Archon's own seal.

'Sorry to have troubled you, lady,' the first soldier said

and the second nodded politely as her papers were handed back. Then they turned to Zoë.

'I don't have any papers,' she said, looking alarmed and turning to Morgan for help. 'I wasn't ever asked for them before.'

'New rule, lady,' the Tetrarchate soldier said sharply. 'As of two days past all citizens are required to show identification for inspection whenever they enter the city.'

'I didn't know,' Zoë stammered and looked back at Morgan again.

'I'll vouch for her,' Morgan said. 'She works for a city merchant I know.' Then when the soldier looked doubtful she added in a confident tone that was becoming more and more natural since she'd met Ciren and Charm: 'Come on, she doesn't look like a Hajhi, does she?'

'I suppose not,' the soldier admitted with a laugh, looking at Zoë's red hair and then finally nodding. 'Very well then. Pass, lady. But go and get yourself some identification. Your merchant should have told you about the new rules.'

'She's been very busy recently,' Zoë said quickly. 'And thank you . . . um . . . sergeant.'

The soldier snapped a salute and he and his companion stepped back from the gate, letting the two girls past and into the mountain fortress.

Morgan felt better once she was inside the city. Going out into the desert had been strange after so long and visiting Weybridge even stranger. But at her side Zoë looked nervous, understandably after the trouble at the gate, and she met Morgan's eyes ruefully.

'Thanks for doing that,' she said. 'You didn't have to.'

'I think maybe I did,' Morgan said slowly. Then she stopped walking and turned to Zoë. 'Look,' she said, 'I know you're going to see Laura but there's something I have to tell you and it's important.'

'OK,' Zoë said. 'What is it?'

They were standing in the middle of an empty street, the market place of Shattershard empty of stalls and most of the shops shuttered. Leading Zoë over to where the street opened into a plaza Morgan sat down on a stone bench at the edge of the square.

'It's complicated,' she said. 'And I really don't have much time. But this might be something you need to know. And something that Laura and Alex should know too so you don't have to worry about keeping it secret.'

Zoë looked at her intently but she didn't say anything and Morgan realized that the other girl really was listening to her this time.

'I've met some people here,' Morgan explained. 'Magicians who only recently arrived in the city.' She chewed on a fingernail for a moment and then went on. 'But they're not from this world at all.'

'There are other worlds?' Zoë's eyes widened and Morgan nodded.

'That's what they told me,' she said. 'They say that there are hundreds of thousands of worlds and just as many Doors between them. They belong to an organization . . . a sort of police force for world-travellers.'

'You're kidding!'

'No, really . . . sort of like that . . . although I'm not explaining it very well . . . But it's called the Collegiate and world-travellers go around making journals of their travels and collecting the books in a Great Library where they all meet up.' She shook her head. 'I still don't understand much of it myself,' she admitted. 'But my friends, Ciren and Charm . . . '

'That's what they're called?' Zoë looked startled. 'Strange names . . . '

'They're strange people,' Morgan admitted. 'Anyway, one of their rules is to help other world-travellers. They tell them about the Collegiate and a list of Doors so if . . . if anything dangerous happens in a world . . . they know how to find the Doors that will take them to another world that's safe.'

'And they told you?' Zoë said.

'They've initiated me,' Morgan told her. 'I'm a member of the Collegiate too now.'

Zoë's face changed when she said that and Morgan waited for the other girl to sneer and was surprised when Zoë turned her grimace into a shrug.

'That sounded kind of creepy,' she said, spreading her hands. 'Like you just joined a cult.'

'It's really hard to explain, Zoë,' Morgan said helplessly. 'I'm not trying to recruit you, OK. I'm just telling you this stuff because I think you should know. And because you can tell the others about it. They won't listen to me.'

'Yeah, that's fair enough.' Zoë nodded. 'OK, sorry. I didn't meant to interrupt.'

'There's not much more of it anyway,' Morgan admitted. 'Just this. If something bad happens in Shattershard. If the Hajhim attack . . . and I think they probably will do soon . . . then there are other Doors on this world.'

Zoë blinked in surprise and Morgan leaned forward, lowering her voice even though there was no one around in the market place.

'One's in the capital city,' she said. 'I don't know where exactly, but it leads to the Great Library . . . that's this place the Collegiate meet at. And there's another under this city . . . '

'Another Door *here*?' Zoë looked incredulous.

'Yes, but it can't be reached,' Morgan told her. 'It's underneath the city at the bottom of a huge water reservoir about forty feet down. Ciren and Charm have no idea where it leads so it's useless, unreachable.'

'That's . . . weird.' Zoë shook her head and Morgan nodded.

'Nowadays I don't know what's normal any more,' she said and Zoë looked away for a second. 'I expect you think I'm mad,' she said defensively and Zoë shook her head.

'No. I don't,' she said seriously. 'I really don't, Morgan. I'm just confused.'

Morgan gave her a sort of half smile.

'Welcome to the club,' she said.

Morgan left soon after mentioning the Doors and Zoë was left on her own on the stone bench as the black-haired girl whisked herself off up a twisting street and was quickly lost to sight. For a moment Zoë had thought of asking if she could go with her but, although they'd been getting on, Morgan was still a stranger to her. If she was honest with herself Zoë felt closer to Jhezra than she did to Morgan, even this new confident Morgan with her stories of hundreds of other worlds and mages called Ciren and Charm.

This Collegiate thing was unnerving and Zoë thought about it as she stood up from the bench and began to climb up the streets of Shattershard. If Morgan's friends were telling the truth, then Laura and Alex might be in a lot of trouble. Zoë somehow doubted that an organization that policed world-travellers would be all that happy about people starting wars. She wasn't too happy about it herself.

As she climbed up the steep streets and steps of Shattershard, she couldn't help noticing that the city was virtually deserted. The shops and stalls that had delighted her on her first visit were gone or closed, house after house had its windows firmly shuttered or boarded up and the public fountains played softly to themselves instead of being surrounded by people stopping for a rest or children splashing each other with gleaming handfuls of water. Twice as she walked up the mountainside Zoë saw squads of soldiers jogging past: those in Shattershard grey obviously outnumbered by the ones in Tetrarchate blue and silver. Trying to look as if she belonged, Zoë didn't meet their eyes.

Many of the streets and bridges had names carved or painted on them and when Zoë eventually reached a stone gargoyle holding out a sign that read 'Treetower' she knew she was getting close to her destination and her chest suddenly felt fluttery with nerves. The Harrells and the Hajhim were planning to attack and Jhezra had been right when she said the people of Shattershard knew it. Morgan knew it too and had placed herself firmly on the other side, unless these Collegiate people counted as a third side entirely.

That thought brought her up to the gate of the Harrells' mansion and Zoë realized belatedly that she still hadn't worked out what she was going to say. But it was too late now and she went into the courtyard and up the stone steps that led to the main entrance. Taking a deep breath she knocked on the door.

11

Zoë had known she was in trouble as soon as Alex opened the door of the mansion. His expression had shifted from shock to annoyance to concern in less than a second and, grabbing her arm, he had virtually hauled her inside.

'What the hell are *you* doing here?' he demanded and Zoë tried to hide her nervousness.

'I want to see Laura,' she told him and Alex rolled his eyes.

'Well, you bloody well can't,' he said. 'Look, why don't you just turn around and go back home, Zoë? Laura can't come out to play right now.'

'Why? Because she's out somewhere spying for you?' Zoë asked hotly, glaring at him, but before Alex could answer a familiar figure strode into the room.

'Iskander . . . could you tell me . . . ' he began before he recognized Zoë. 'Jzohee?' he said, puzzled, looking from her to Alex and back again. 'What are you doing here?'

'You *know* her?' Alex virtually screeched the question and Tzandrian blinked.

'Jzohee was in the desert two days ago,' Tzandrian admitted. 'Jhezra said she was a friend of yours.'

'Jhezra!' Alex shouted. Then he turned away from Zoë and set off through the door Tzandrian had come in from. 'Watch her!' he ordered over his shoulder as he took off at a run.

Zoë and Tzandrian looked at each other and the Hajhi boy put his hand on his dagger.

'You stay there, Jzohee,' he said. 'Do you have a weapon?'

'No, I'm not a soldier,' Zoë told him. 'Or a warrior. Or whatever.' Her hands felt awkward dangling at her sides but she didn't move from the spot.

'Then we have no problem.' Tzandrian didn't take his hand from his dagger but his stance was relaxed, continuing to watch her almost politely.

They didn't have to wait for long until Alex and Jhezra arrived back up the stairs and faced her. Alex's expression was a little calmer but Jhezra was frowning.

'I warned you it was dangerous to return to the city,' Jhezra said when she saw Zoë. 'Please understand that I wish this was not necessary.' Zoë blanched at that and Jhezra flashed her a suddenly bright smile. 'No, my friend,' she said in a softer voice. 'Do not fear. No harm comes to you from us.'

'Of course not,' Alex said hurriedly. 'Don't be an idiot. No one's going to hurt you.'

'It is simply that too much is known to you now,' Jhezra told her. 'For the safety of my own people it would be best that you remain at our side until the battle is finished.' She paused. 'And for your safety also,' she added.

'Then I'm in protective custody,' Zoë said bitterly.

Glancing at Alex she asked, 'Can I see Laura now then?'

'She's not here,' he said shortly. 'You had better come with us . . . and stay quiet.'

Jhezra and Tzandrian had escorted her into the room she was now in, and after the first couple of hours of waiting, watching the Hajhim talking together and playing a gambling game with stone pebbles, Tzandrian had brought her a cup of water and a piece of flat-bread. But otherwise she'd been ignored. She recognized Vaysha among the other six Hajhi warriors but the scout hadn't shown any recognition when her narrow eyes slid across Zoë alone in her corner.

Sitting cross-legged in the corner of the large basement room, Zoë bit her lips and said nothing. She'd stopped silently cursing herself for her stupidity some hours before and now she just sat and watched the preparations being made around her. The Hajhim went about their business methodically, arming themselves with familiar ease before collecting their share of the objects stacked separately on the racks at the side of the room: an array of short cylinders wrapped tightly with rags and tied up with string.

On the other side of the room Alex and Jhezra talked quietly, Alex glancing at his watch every now and again. The tension in the room was palpable and when the door swung open quietly everyone glanced over at the new arrival before turning back to their work. Dressed in a floor length mulberry-coloured dress trimmed with frothing lace, Laura looked incongruous in a gathering where almost everyone else wore subdued browns and bristled with weaponry. Zoë watched as Laura crossed the room and joined Alex but her classmate didn't so much as glance at her.

Now the Hajhim were evidently suiting up for the battle and one by one they gathered their weapons and their cargo of cylinders, two or three to a person, before moving out of the room. It didn't take much imagination to guess what the objects were. Bombs, Zoë had decided, maybe Molotov cocktails or incendiaries or whatever it was that terrorists and freedom fighters used. The barrels stacked by the catapults in the war-camp were probably more of the same kind of thing. She wondered briefly how they had been made but she was certain that the ingredients had come from Earth, probably in the same load as Alex's purchases of stationery and Tai Kwon Do manuals.

As the Hajhim filed out, Alex carefully oversaw their distribution of cylinders, before finally taking two of his own. It wasn't until then that he turned to Zoë and Jhezra and Laura crossed the room to join him.

'Oh, so you remembered me, then,' Zoë said, getting awkwardly to her feet and trying to ignore the pins and needles in her legs. 'What next? What are you going to do with me while you're off blowing up bits of the city?'

'Zoë, relax,' Laura said, her expression earnest. 'There's a lot you don't know about what's going on.'

'Because you didn't tell me!' Zoë said, unable to believe the way Laura was acting as if everything was normal.

'I didn't want to get you involved in all this,' Laura said, gesturing with a casual hand at the rack on which the bombs had been stacked. Zoë bit her lip and tried to stay calm.

'Well, I'm involved now,' she said, glancing from Laura to Jhezra and Alex.

'Unfortunately,' Alex said grimly. Jhezra didn't say anything but her dark eyes were thoughtful.

'Yes, you're involved,' Laura agreed reasonably. 'So we're letting you into the plan.'

Zoë resisted the urge to point out that she already knew or guessed most of the plan already, it wasn't the time for bravado, and waited to hear what Laura would come up with.

'Alex and Jhezra are joining the rest of the army,' Laura said. 'And you don't need to know their part of the plan.' Her pale green eyes were as cool and clear as her voice as she continued: 'But I'll be going to a safer place than this. Once the battle is joined anything could happen in the city and it's not safe for me to stay here or for us to leave you here either.'

'OK,' Zoë said, trying not to betray her thoughts.

'So I think it would be best if you come with me,' Laura told her. 'But you have to promise that you won't make any trouble. Just stay close to me and keep quiet until the battle's over.'

'All right,' Zoë said, shrugging uncomfortably. 'It's not as if I have much choice, is it?'

'Good,' Laura said but Jhezra's liquid eyes met Zoë's gently.

'It is a hard thing to ask of you, I know,' she said quietly. 'But it is best for all of us this way and . . . ' she nodded, 'you are right, there are no other choices left.'

Alex gradually felt the annoyance Zoë's arrival had caused beginning to fade. Mostly he'd been upset with Jhezra for not telling him that the younger girl had been wandering about in the desert with the Hajhim. But when Laura came back from checking on some last-minute information the problem had been solved and he didn't doubt that his sister was capable of keeping an eye on her red-headed friend.

While evening was settling in over the streets of Shattershard, Alex and the Hajhim took a darker road, leaving the residence by means of a twisted staircase in a corner of the mansion's basement. Accompanied by the steady churning noise of water gushing through the pipes and channels around them they walked steadily along the corridors scooped out of the mountain rock. Altogether there were nine of them strung out along the passage with Alex and Jhezra in the lead and Vaysha and Tzandrian at the rear.

Unlike the deeper tunnels below and the chutes and pipes of the sewers, these passages were in reasonable repair, and they kept silent in case they encountered some servant or worker in the twisting passages. But they saw no one, and as their path began to climb again Alex drew in a silent sigh of relief and used his lantern to shine a light on his watch.

'We're on time,' he said softly to Jhezra. 'And we're close to the place now.'

'Good then.' His girlfriend nodded and turned to pass the message softly back along the line. As the others tightened up their formation, a few more steps brought Alex into a wide chamber where the noise of gushing water echoed hollowly from the walls.

Alex looked around in satisfaction. This was the place he and Jhezra had discovered four months past. This was the chamber where the gate-locking mechanism intersected with the water system of the fortress city. Hydraulic power, based on the motive force of water, opened and shut those massive stone gates like the chambers of a canal lock. In the towers to either side of them were massive wheels that the guards turned at night to control a system of sluices between massive water tanks that held the gates shut or allowed them to open. It was an elegant system and Alex had been pleased with himself for working it out. But it was Jhezra who had asked, when he first explained it, what would happen if the water supply was cut off and it was that question that had led them to look for this place.

They were beneath the gates here, far below the actual lock mechanism for the doors, which was heavily guarded by the Shattershard militia and now by Tetrarchate troops. This plain stone chamber had no significance whatsoever to the gate guards but it lay next to one of the main channels that sent water into and out of the locking mechanism. Along one wall of the chamber was the pile of round barrels they had placed there earlier that day and Alex checked quickly that they hadn't been disturbed. The smell of oil from their cloth covering was pungent and Alex tried to breathe shallowly as he went over his preparations.

'I feel like Guy Fawkes,' he said under his breath as Jhezra came to join him and shook his head when she looked curious. 'Nothing,' he said. 'Everything's set.'

'Very well then,' Jhezra said. 'I'll tell the others to be ready.'

The rest of the Hajhim moved back out of the chamber to the foot of a nearby staircase leading up. This was the most dangerous part of the plan. When the barrels exploded the wall would collapse in on the water pipe: creating a blockage that would cut off the water supply to the gates. When that happened they would need to get out of these tunnels fast as water filled the rooms and chambers around the broken pipe.

Taking his matches from his pocket Alex stepped back from the barrels and lit a long stave of prepared wood. It caught easily and he glanced back at Jhezra, standing ready at the chamber entrance. His heart was beating fast with excitement and he grinned at her a bit wildly and saw her smile tightly back. Taking a deep shuddering breath Alex glanced once more at his watch and then heard the sound he'd been listening for. Floating down through the stone walls of the chamber came the clanging of a sonorous bell.

'Now!' Jhezra said but Alex was already moving, stroking the burning stave of wood across the oil-soaked covering of the barrels. Flames leapt up across it instantly, licking up and down with terrifying speed in a sudden wave of heat. Alex threw the remains of the stave into the conflagration and staggered back away from the fire, running to join Jhezra at the archway.

'Get going,' he gasped out as he reached her and she didn't wait any longer, racing ahead of him to the stairway.

'Vaysha! Go!' she shouted ahead of them and he saw shadows leaping and twisting ahead from the lanterns the warriors carried as they raced up the stairway.

Jhezra paused for a half beat on the staircase, long enough for Alex to pass her, and then they were climbing the stone steps. Alex took them two at a time, watching his footing as best he could in the flickering lamplight. Above them the bell continued to clang its warning note and Alex almost stumbled as he came to the top of the staircase and up into the long sloping corridor above. Jhezra fell heavily against him and they staggered together just as a loud boom erupted from beneath the stairs and the walls of the corridor trembled and shook. Stones shook loose from the ceiling and Jhezra sprang to her feet, hauling Alex up after her.

'Run, Iskander!' she shouted in his ear and they flew down the passageway. Alex's muscles screamed as he forced himself to run faster and his lungs burned as he tried to gasp in air. Shielding his head with his right arm from the pebbles raining down on them, he skidded round the last bend of the corridor and up and out into the suddenly sharp air.

As the bell clanged and echoed across the city, reverberating along the walls of the mountain, the tower guards set the wheels in motion to close the gate. The evening sky was a bruised blue violet and on the battlements the soldiers watching the desert relaxed at the sound of the evening bell, listening for the dull booming noise of the stone gates shutting tight.

It didn't come. As the chimes of the bell died away there was a rumbling noise from the rock, as if the bones of the mountain were protesting about something, a grumbling that grew rapidly to a roar of noise before dying down beneath the edge of hearing. In the gateway the heavy slabs of the stone gates shivered slightly and stilled in their open position.

It was then that the Hajhim attacked. The Tetrarchate patrols that roamed the desert had been too predictable in their routines and from concealment in the sand dunes the Hajhi scouts had struck under the cover of twilight. The city guards on the towers had no way of knowing that the desert was not being watched that night; their first sign that something was wrong was the shuddering of the gates. As the roar of sound died from the mountain it was succeeded by a rushing thunder from the desert as the Hajhim army rose up out of the darkness and stormed towards the gates.

Frantically lifting arrows to bows and shouting alarms, the tower guards tried to halt their advance. But before the first arrow could be loosed a heavy object struck the left tower, hurled upwards from the shadowy throng of warriors, and exploded into a fireball of destructive heat. Two more followed it, hitting the right tower and a section of parapet, and the shouts from the battlements turned into screams.

Already the first wave of Hajhi riders had passed through the gate, striking left and right with their scimitars as the gate guards rushed to defend their posts. Behind them the next wave swept over the remaining guards as the bell lifted its voice for the second time that evening in a peal of urgent alarm that clattered and clanged back and forth across the mountain heights. The streets of Shattershard were a mêlée of churning horses' hooves and wildly swinging scimitars, platoons of guardsmen forming knots back to back as they attempted to stem the flow of Hajhim pouring through the open gates.

On the other side of the mountain fortress, beacons blazed into light on the towers of the Archon's palace and guards rushed to secure the entrances. In the public rooms the courtiers rushed to the windows and balconies, deafened by the urgent appeal of the alarm bells and staring in horror at the fireballs erupting on the opposite side of the mountain, shouting each other down as they struggled for an explanation.

In the audience chamber the senior advisers rose in a hubbub of confusion and the Archon's bodyguards, Athen and Edren, took immediate positions on either side of their lord. Gripping the arms of his throne tightly, Kal had to raise his voice as loud as he could to be heard above the crowd as a tall figure arrived suddenly in the room.

'General Shirishath!' he shouted, drowning out the querulous voices of the advisers. 'Your report!'

As his words penetrated, the voices died down and advisers and courtiers turned towards the newcomer for an explanation.

'Lord Archon, the Hajhim have attacked in force,' the general announced in stark tones. 'My troops are rushing to repel the attack but there is a pitched battle in the streets about the city gate.' He bowed low and finished: 'Your militia and personal guard can best protect your highness here. With due respect I must leave now to join my troops in defending your city.'

'Your damned troops have brought this upon us!' Cardinal Jagannath's voice rose up above the multitude, trembling with anger as the old man rose shakily to his feet. 'Curse you and your Tetrarch!'

'No.' Kal put his hand on Jagannath's arm, forcing him back into his seat. 'This is the hand of our enemy. He has finally struck.' He looked down at the tall figure of the general and nodded to him. 'Go where you wish. I will join the defenders at the palace gate,' he said and stepped down from his throne.

'No, Lord Archon, I beg of you!' Jagannath looked horrified. 'The danger . . . '

'Is mine to risk,' Kal told him. Untying the drawstring of his cloak he dropped its white gold fabric on the abandoned throne and unsheathed the length of his sword. 'Now,' he said. 'Let us see who our enemy really is.'

Courtiers fell back as the Archon stalked down the dais steps, his naked sword in his hand and his face set grim with intent, and Athen and Edren hastened to follow his lead as he strode through the double doors of the Audience Hall.

'My lord Archon,' Athen called after him. 'Please wait . . . '

Kal slowed his steps a little, going down a curving staircase, and his bodyguards caught up with him halfway down.

'My lord,' Edren said breathlessly, sliding his sword from its sheath. 'You should seek safety.'

'Yes, Lord Archon,' Athen agreed. 'Let us escort you to your rooms.'

Kal didn't look at either of them, walking swiftly and surely down the spiralling stairs, his own grip tight on his sword.

'I don't think so,' he said. 'Our people are fighting and dying out there in the streets. Shirishath can lead his troops, I'm going to lead mine . . . even if it's the last thing I ever do.' At the base of the steps he paused at the entrance to the public halls. 'I release you from your service,' he said. 'Since I no longer wish to be protected.'

'Very well, my lord,' Athen said and bowed, drawing his sword and holding it ready. 'Lead us as you would.'

Kal blinked and Edren nodded on his other side.

'Lead on, Kal,' he said. 'Wherever you choose. It just so happens we're going the same way.'

'As you will,' Kal said, accepting their decision, and strode on down the stairs and out of the palace.

From the roof of the magician's guild-house halfway up the central crater of the mountain city, Charm and Ciren looked down at the battlefield of the streets. Flashes of light erupted in the midst of the combat followed by the dull boom of explosions, and figures reeled back from the leaping flames.

Ciren's eyes were glazed as he stood in a trance, Charm's hand steadying his shoulder, and he came back to himself with a shiver.

'There's death in those streets,' he said, meeting his twin's violet eyes. 'The attackers are using weapons of brimstone and power that explode into flame when they're thrown.'

'Other-world weaponry.' Charm stared down over the

parapet into the chaos below. 'This has been carefully planned.'

'Not carefully enough,' Ciren said grimly. 'Look there.'

His twin followed his gesture and looked across the city in the direction of the palace. On the higher buildings and towers of the mountainside Tetrarchate troops were taking defensive positions. Drawing a spyglass from his belt Ciren focused on the soldiers and repeated what he saw in clear steady tones:

'Squads are moving to block the main thoroughfares up towards the palace and the troops on the battlements are pulling back to towers halfway along the mountain's rim. The ground troops are armed with sabres but the tower guards have crossbows . . . ' He paused. 'They haven't shot yet, they're waiting for the Hajhi riders to get higher up.'

Charm had turned as he spoke and was facing in the other direction, looking down at the conflict in the streets.

'I think the Hajhim have taken the gate,' she said, raising her voice to be heard over the erupting explosions. 'There's no sign of resistance there and the towers are burning. The battle has expanded around the lower streets of the city and the militia have formed pockets of resistance. Fires are burning in some of the buildings and some of the bridges have collapsed. Some of the city guard are retreating to higher streets and towers. The Hajhim are bringing their catapults in through the gate . . . '

'What's the range on the catapults?' Ciren called from the other end of the roof. 'Do they rank crossbows?'

'They have a good distance but the force is poorly directed,' Charm called back. 'Some of those brimstone barrels are landing among their own warriors.'

Ciren snapped shut his spyglass and rejoined Charm by the parapet, unshouldering the bow he wore and stringing it.

'I have the book,' he said, adjusting the straps on the light pack he carried and tying his cloak back to display the archer's vambraces on his forearms. 'What's our best direction?'

'The gate is impassable for now but if the Hajhim take the city they will drop their defences there,' Charm said, moving nearer to him to be heard. 'The conflict on the ground moves closer towards us and the Tetrarchate are preparing to meet them halfway. Waiting the battle out is a possible option but risky if the battle comes down these streets. Going higher up the city puts us in range of the Tetrarchate crossbows.'

'Morgan is almost certainly at the Archon's palace,' Ciren reminded her. 'And the Tetrarchate troops will recognize us as friends.'

'Upwards then,' Charm said and unsheathed her two swords in a smooth motion. 'Be wary,' she told her twin and her lips set in a grim smile.

Zoë flattened herself against the wall as a knot of courtiers pressed past her on to the balcony. Laura, beside her, kept a tight grip on her arm as the crowd pushed them out of the way.

'Watch out,' she whispered to Zoë. 'If this lot panics it could turn into a riot in here. We should try and find somewhere more out of the way.'

'Whatever you say,' Zoë said under her breath as Laura led her out of the scrum, keeping a hold on Zoë's hand as she worked her way round the edge of the room.

No one seemed to notice them, all pressing to the windows of the public hall to discover the progress of the battle. The cries of elation and disappointment from the watchers reminded Zoë in a gruesome way of people at a fireworks display.

Laura paused at a clear place behind the abandoned tables of food and drink and let go of Zoë's hand.

'Stay close to me, Zoë,' she said. 'If we lose each other we might not find each other again.'

'Don't worry,' Zoë assured her. 'I'm right behind you.' She smiled reassuringly at Laura. Then, when the other girl turned her back, she clenched her hands into fists.

She couldn't believe that Laura was pretending they were in this together, but the hell of this was that Zoë didn't have any choice but to stick with her. She felt tense with anger and fear as she followed Laura through the halls, skirting the edge of the crowds, and she forced herself to breathe slowly and deeply. Being angry wasn't going to help now, she told herself, just concentrate on getting through this alive.

Alex ducked back into an alleyway as a flaming missile burst on the roof of a nearby house, sending masonry flying and raining down chips of burning wood into the street. Hurrying back to his companions, he was in time to see two of them hurl their firebombs into a clutch of guardsmen rounding the bottom end of the alley. Scimitars spun as the Hajhim hurled themselves after the bombs and Alex groaned as they reeled back out of the clouds of smoke, coughing and spluttering.

Catching sight of him, Jhezra and Vaysha hurried to his side, followed by Tzandrian and two other warriors.

'The rest?' Alex asked and Jhezra shook her head.

'We were hard pressed,' she said. 'I think we're in the thick of the battle here.'

'We've got to get past it!' Alex said anxiously. 'The plan is for us to get to the palace.'

'The plan!' Vaysha glared at him. 'This is a battle, Iskander. Don't plan. Fight!'

'She's right,' Jhezra said, meeting his eyes. 'We've lost people and we don't know the way the war is going. We must move on and try to meet up with more warriors who can reinforce us.'

'All right,' Alex said. 'But let's try to move higher up and out of this. The catapults are shooting this part of the city to blazes.'

'Yes,' Tzandrian agreed suddenly. 'And on foot the riders might mistake us for the guards in grey.'

'Well said,' Jhezra nodded. 'On then.'

Together they went back up the alley and into the street beyond. The second storey of the building hit by the missile had slid into the street and the neighbouring houses were ablaze. As Alex stared, holding his scimitar slackly in his hand, Jhezra slammed his shoulder hard.

'Stay focused,' she told him, pushing him ahead of her up the street. 'Watch my back.' Raising her voice she called out loud, 'Vaysha, scout forward! Tzan! Hold the rear. You two with me and Iskander. Quickly now!'

The other warriors hurried to their positions, flanking them as the group moved on up the street, and Alex glanced briefly at Jhezra. She opened her mouth to say something and her words were drowned out by a sudden deep rumble in the rock below.

'Down!' Vaysha shouted from the front and they crouched low to the ground as a groaning noise echoed from one side of the mountain to the other, shuddering through the depths of Shattershard. Already unstable buildings in the city below crashed and blazed into the stone streets and a hot wind brought them the sound of horses screaming.

'What's happening?' Jhezra asked, as they staggered to their feet again.

'Earthquake?' Alex suggested, raising his voice to be heard, but her eyes were uncomprehending.

The earth shook again and they forced themselves upright on the shaking roadway, following Vaysha's lead as she indicated up the next turn of the road. From beneath the stone road came a tumbling rumble and Alex eyed the mountainside with misgiving. It sounded as if the earth were trying to tear itself apart. Beside him Jhezra gripped his hand suddenly and her dark eyes met his with an abrupt fear.

'Iskander,' she said. 'What have we done?'

12

Morgan glanced quickly about her as she made her way out through the courtyard entrance and towards the palace gates. She'd arrived at the Audience Hall to find Kal already gone and the advisers in a state of confusion. The first explosions had come while she waited in the roof garden and at first she hadn't been able to believe what she was seeing. At first she'd wondered if it was some kind of magical attack causing the blast of fire that rocketed through the sky. Then a sudden blaze of light cast the scene into sharp relief and she'd recognized the missiles as bombs.

Coming down a short run of steps Morgan lost her balance as a succession of shuddering tremors shook the palace as if a series of earthquakes were racking the city. Landing on hands and knees on the hard stone she gasped for breath as the mountain juddered and rocked, finally pulling herself upright again on a fallen piece of masonry. A cluster of courtiers spilled out ahead of her into the courtyard and a handful of the palace guards hastened to join their comrades on the carved rock walls of the palace defences. On the wall itself Morgan caught sight of a slim straight figure wearing a white-gold crown and she hurried towards him, slipping and sliding on the heaving flagstones.

'Kal!' she called out across the space between them and managed to regain her footing just as she arrived at the wall.

'Morgan, thank the gods.' With a sudden gasp of relief Kal pulled her into a recklessly tight hug with his left arm while his right hand kept a close grip on his sword.

'What's happening?' she asked, her eyes wide as she stared past him at the flares of light and leaping shadows in the streets below.

'The Hajhim have attacked in force,' he told her. 'They have weapons . . . ' He shook his head. 'Weapons I've not seen before, but they explode into flame, burning and destroying buildings and soldiers alike.'

Morgan bit her lips; the truth didn't seem to matter very much now, but all the same she had to say it.

'They have weapons like this where I come from . . . ' she whispered, meeting his grey eyes flinchingly. 'I'm sorry . . . They must have been brought here by people I know.'

Kal looked down at her searchingly. 'Did you know about this, Morgan?' he asked. Despite the devastation of the battle all his attention was focused on her. 'Are you on their side?'

'No!' She shook her head quickly. 'I promise, I didn't know. If I'd realized . . . ' She shuddered as another explosion heaved up from the streets and lit up the night with a sudden flash. 'I'm on your side,' she promised him. 'No one else's.'

'I trust you,' Kal said and took her hand in his. 'But

my side isn't a very safe place to be right now.' Another earthquake shook the walls as he spoke and his grip tightened on her arm to steady her.

'Where is?' Morgan asked breathlessly, clinging to her prince's arm. 'I'm staying. Even if my magic isn't good for much . . . ' she added and then tried for a joke. 'Maybe just *seeing* a black mage will scare the Hajhim off?'

'They'll write sagas about us,' Kal agreed drily. 'The boy Archon and his lover the black mage . . . whose enemies perished from fear at the sight of them.'

Morgan blushed at that and Kal laughed, kissing her quickly and lightly before turning back to his bodyguards, who'd been maintaining a careful watch on the battle below.

'You've seen Morgan before,' Kal told them. 'If anything happens to me . . . do your best to see her safe.'

The young guards looked at each other and then Athen bowed politely.

'It will be an honour,' he said but before Morgan could say it was Kal who needed protecting, went on to add: 'But with the best will in the world it may not be possible, my lord.'

Kal frowned and Edren nodded.

'He's right, Kal,' he said. 'Since anything that happens to you will have found us in the way.'

'You . . . ' Kal blinked at the sincerity in his bodyguards' eyes.

'And me,' Morgan added. 'So I wouldn't need any protecting afterwards.'

'All right then.' Kal gave in. 'I should probably say something very poetic and noble but I can't think of anything better than . . . thank you, my friends.'

They stood looking at each other for another moment then a crash from the streets nearby turned their attention back to the wall. But as they took their positions Morgan heard Edren add drily:

'Never mind, we can write the poetry after we've won.'

Alex battled his way up through the smoke and flames. All around him the battle had degenerated into chaos. Tetrarchic troops and Hajhi warriors struggled together here and there in the streets and at the remaining towers but all over the city the conflict was splitting up into smaller knots and eddies as the balance of the battle collapsed into stalemate.

Alex's own scimitar was wet with blood and he couldn't remember how it had got that way. Half the time he'd been running blind, trying to shield his eyes from the clouds of smoke and ash, hacking with his scimitar when their little group had run into soldiers with eyes as wild as their own. Beneath his feet the rumblings of the rock continued ominously: the complex hydraulic system of water courses breaking free from their usual channels as explosion after explosion forced them out of their customary paths. Everything was out of control and Alex came to a gasping halt, his heart hammering in his ears as loud as the mountain's groans, leaning on his scimitar for support.

'Iskander!' someone shouted and he shook his head to clear it, meeting Jhezra's eyes as she stared into his face. 'This way,' she said, helping him to stand.

Dragging his sleeve across his face Alex blinked dust out of his eyes and looked at his companions. He, Jhezra, Vaysha, and Tzandrian were standing near to a crumbling bridge halfway up the bowl of the mountain. Somehow they'd managed to get out of the thick of the battle and looking around Alex realized he recognized this area.

'The battle goes badly,' Jhezra said, her eyes dark as she studied the progress of the fighting below them.

'What should we do, Iskander?' Tzandrian asked and Alex choked back a sense of hysteria.

He closed his eyes, trying desperately to think, and then he heard Vaysha's voice say, 'Now is the time for the plan, Iskander.' He opened his eyes to see her pointing up the mountain to where the Archon's palace jutted out of the cliffside. 'You said we should get to the palace.' She gestured. 'Behold. Here it is.'

'Yes.' Alex struggled to remember what he'd intended. 'The palace . . . ' He looked up at its elaborately carved outer walls, searching for a way to salvage victory from the ruins of his plan, and saw the tiny number of guards left to protect it. Slowly he nodded. 'The Archon will be there,' he said. 'If we can capture him . . . '

'He will order the soldiers to surrender.' Jhezra nodded her understanding.

'Then what are we waiting for?' Tzandrian asked, raising his scimitar.

Ciren and Charm moved swiftly through Shattershard, skirting the edges of the battle. Ciren decided their route, his mind open to the emanations of power. The taste of the brimstone weapons of the invaders was recognizable as it tore through the atmospheric magics of the air with a choking waft of oily smoke. Locked in their deadly struggle, the fighters didn't notice the blond twins moving calmly through the conflict, keeping their balance as the ground shook beneath their feet.

Once more they had taken to the rooftops. Now that the streets were full of broken stone it was as good a route as any and they'd made it to a point where they could survey the tangle of streets around and about the palace.

'Look there,' Ciren said, pointing, and Charm followed his gesture to where a group of figures stood at the top of the palace walls. Two young guards flanked the crowned figure of the Archon and the girl in black at his side.

'Our missing companion seems to have gone native,' Charm said, her violet eyes studying the tableau ahead of them.

'King-makers,' Ciren said quietly. 'You were right, twin, world-travellers are king-makers every one.'

'King-makers and king-breakers,' Charm answered him, directing his gaze to a small group of armed warriors making their way up the street to the palace gates. At their head was a tall boy whose curly hair was a dark brown instead of the glossy black of his Hajhi companions, dressed in an outlandish coat and carrying an unsheathed scimitar. Charm's mouth curved into a gentle smile as she watched him and Ciren frowned.

'What thoughts do you have?' he asked.

'Of kingship and domination,' Charm said, still smiling. 'Of weapons brought from world to world and Doors opening to let armies through.' She looked back at Ciren and the smile slowly faded from her face. 'We all crave power,' she reminded him.

'True enough,' her twin admitted. 'So what now?'

The mountain shuddered beneath their feet in answer to his question and the twins balanced quickly as the roof they were standing on rocked ominously.

'We must leave here,' Charm said simply. 'We've discovered what we needed to. These misguided world-travellers present no threat to our masters and the world they come from must be reported.' A crash shook the air and she raised her voice to add, 'And I think they'll be interested to know of these weapons.'

Ciren shuddered suddenly and bowed his head.

'Very well then,' he said. 'But we must try to bring Morgan with us . . . our oath demands . . . '

'I don't contest it,' Charm agreed. 'I'd argue that we should try to bring the other world-travellers also but since they seem to have been using this city to play war games I doubt we can salvage them.'

'King-makers all.' Ciren's face set suddenly. 'I wish just once we could meet a world-traveller who wasn't obsessed by power.'

'Be careful what you wish for, twin!' Charm replied instantly. 'We are agents of the Wheel and our faction thinks of altruism as a threat. If we did meet someone unmotivated by the desire for power it would be because we were ordered to eliminate them.'

As the walls of the palace trembled and shook, the light globes in the ceilings crashed together, spattering into tiny explosions of golden sparks. Mosaic pieces came loose from the ornamented pillars and scattered into chips on the stone floor. Laura and Zoë picked their way past the wreckage and the shaking groups of courtiers, eyeing the shuddering roof with concern.

'This place sounds like it's going to fall in,' Laura said, and added under her breath, 'What's Alex *doing* out there?'

Zoë eyed her with dislike but held in her comments. Instead she let her voice rise high with the air of panic:

'Laura, we have to get out of here. I think the roof's going to fall in!'

'All right, calm down,' Laura said, glancing back over her shoulder with a superior expression. 'There's an exit this way.'

'Please hurry!' Zoë pleaded but her mind was quickly assessing her chances of escaping from Laura outside. As

Zoë followed her out into the palace courtyard, any ideas of escape fell away when she looked out at the city and saw a war zone.

Shattershard was ablaze; flames licked up the sides of the falling buildings and shadowy figures fought each other up and down the steep streets. Metal clashed and screamed as swords clanged together and all around her the mountain was groaning and shaking. Covering her ears with her hands to block out the gut-wrenching noise, she stumbled across the courtyard after Laura.

The scene was apocalyptic and Zoë wondered for one last moment if any of this could really be happening. Then a crash of stone brought her out of her daze and she realized that the walls of the palace were slipping and sliding, the defenders at the walls losing their balance as they fell from a sickening height over the edge of the battlements.

'What's happening?' Laura demanded angrily. 'Why is the mountain shaking like this?'

'Probably something to do with your bombs,' Zoë yelled back raggedly. 'And your stupid war . . . ' She glared at Laura with impotent rage, shaking her head. 'Why did you have to do it, Laura? You found another world and you . . . you've *broken* it.' Hot tears sprang from her eyes and she ignored them. 'And now we're probably going to die here,' she finished, 'right in the middle of your bloody stupid war! I hope you go to hell, Laura Harrell!'

Laura looked at her in amazement but as Zoë finished speaking the expression in her pale green eyes had shifted into contempt.

'How ungrateful,' she said coldly. 'Fine then, if that's the way you think . . . get out of my sight.'

Kal sought for balance on the shifting stone of the square

as he saw the Hajhim warriors arrive at the gate. At their head was a face he recognized, a pretended merchant trader who now carried a Hajhi scimitar in his hand, the face of his enemy. Struggling to control his anger he moved into a fighting stance as Morgan, Athen, and Edren took their places at his side.

Alex stepped forward, lifting his scimitar, and Kal moved smoothly in to block his path. The metal weapons slid against each other in a grinding judder before breaking apart again and with a shout the Hajhim and the Archon's guards hurled themselves forward into the fight.

'Surrender!' Alex shouted as his eyes met Kal's across their blades. 'You've lost. Tell the Tetrarchate troops to give up.'

'They don't obey my orders, you fool,' Kal told him grimly. 'They never did.' He sliced hard at the taller boy's face, causing him to flinch back, before flicking a long cut down his sword arm. 'The Tetrarchate don't care about this city any more than you do, traitor.' With a clang he knocked Alex's scimitar flying and raised his sword for the *coup de grâce* only to face another weapon as Jhezra leapt to defend Alex.

'Fight me, not him!' she said, her sickle-shaped dagger flashing forward as her scimitar caught and held his sword. 'Stay back!'

Seeing the dagger curve past Kal's defence and into his chest Athen shouted out loud, ignoring his own opponent as he tried to hurl himself past the Hajhi warrior to defend his lord. Tzandrian's scimitar whistled through the air, slicing deep into the bodyguard's chest, and stuck there while three palace guards fell on Tzandrian from behind, cutting him down as he attempted to defend himself with his dagger. On the other side of the gate Vaysha saw him fall and slashed her way to his side, her blades whirling and dancing as she carved her way through the defenders, and was brought to a halt as Edren stepped into her path. Carrying Athen's sword as well as his own he slashed wildly with his left arm and Vaysha stepped back, only to have him step forward neatly and run his own sword into her chest. Her scimitar, still raised for the attack, swept downwards as she died and brought Edren down with her in a grisly embrace.

Morgan screamed as she saw Kal stagger, his left arm clutching at his side as blood spread across his chest, and leapt forward to help him. A hand caught suddenly in her hair and pulled her roughly back and she struggled, whirling round to see a familiar face looking at her with contempt.

'Stay out of it,' Laura told her coolly, still holding on to her hair. 'Don't get in the way.'

'You!' Morgan ripped loose with a sudden wrench, ignoring the pain. 'I warned you, Laura,' she said, raising her hands in an ominous gesture. 'You didn't listen to me.' Taking a deep breath she concentrated her magic and began to draw in her power.

'Give it up, Morgan,' Laura said with a shrug. 'You don't impress me.'

Focusing her mind on her spell, Morgan ignored her. Laura had never really believed in the magic of Shattershard. But Morgan could sense its power in the back of her mind as a force to be drawn upon. Laura's words fuelled Morgan's spell as she concentrated on her hatred and bitterness and hurled them out at Laura, seeing the magic erupt in black fire from her fingers to engulf Laura in darkness.

Zoë watched in horror as the palace guards and Hajhi warriors fought and died, falling to her knees as the earth shook in great heaving motions beneath her. In the gateway Kal and Jhezra alone were left standing, fighting backwards and forwards as the stone walls of the palace shed chunks of masonry into the courtyard.

Lifting her eyes beyond the palace Zoë could see that great sections of towering parapets were sliding down the sides of the mountain and into the stepped streets below. Spires shivered and towers crumbled as the mountain rumbled its complaint. In the gate Kal and Jhezra fell apart, both bleeding heavily, as the courtyard suddenly lifted up like a cat arching its back and threw them into the air. Zoë fell with bruising force and was picked up and hurled through the air again as the palace finally finished shaking itself to pieces, sinking into its own foundations as a great hole opened up down the middle of the courtyard.

On the other side she saw Morgan for one last moment, running across the collapsing courtyard to Kal's side. Then the palace of Shattershard fell in like a sandcastle and Zoë found herself falling into a deep pit.

As the palace broke apart beneath him Kal felt a slender figure suddenly attach itself to him, supporting his weight and half-dragging him out of the gates. His arm went around her automatically as she forced him down the falling road, fingers tangling in a length of silky hair.

'Morgan,' he whispered. 'Stop . . . it's useless.' But she couldn't hear him over the sound of Shattershard shaking the buildings loose from the mountainside. Then, as his knees buckled helplessly, an impossible vision appeared at the end of the street. Two black-clad figures came riding across the rocky path on the backs of mountain ponies, identical pointed faces staring down at him and Morgan.

Ciren slid off his pony and pushed Morgan towards it, gesturing for her to mount up.

'Kal first!' she shouted and the fair-haired boy hesitated for only an instant before helping Kal up on to the pony's back instead. Morgan swung herself up after him as Ciren ran to join his twin on the other animal. Then another earthquake shook the street and the ponies leapt forward, racing around the edge of the crater bowl across to the great arch of the city gate.

Behind them buildings continued to crash and burn, smashing their way down the mountainside to tear whole streets in their wake, avalanching down to the base of the crater. Great gouts of flame licked up from the ruins as rivers of water spurted out of the bowels of the mountain to gush in torrents down the twisting streets, and huge holes opened up in the ground like a vision of hell, and the ponies surged frantically towards the gate.

The final quake of Shattershard's walls falling inwards thundered a death shout as the ponies escaped the collapsing mountain. Clouds of dust and smoke rose up as the city gave a last desperate heave and fell back in a sagging tumble of ruined rock.

Buried deep beneath the palace Zoë felt the mountain fall in with a conclusive roar, trapping her beneath tons and tons of stone. Her hands over her head she crouched in the rubble and darkness waiting for the ceiling to fall in and finally bury her alive in the pit.

It didn't happen. The last thunder of the falling mountain settled slowly into silence: a deep conclusive silence like being inside a tomb. Zoë bit the inside of her mouth to stop herself from screaming and waited for her body to stop shaking. It took some time.

Eventually she uncurled herself enough to fumble through the pockets of her coat and find the smooth metal shape of the Zippo lighter. It clicked open and then, when she spun the wheel, flared into enough light to show her a tunnel ahead of her, its floor covered with rough fragments of rock. Her arms and legs were scraped and bleeding and her chest ached painfully as she got to her hands and knees and crawled forward over the edifice of broken stone. Her hands touched a body and she flinched away, expecting it to be one of the dead guards, before she looked down and saw Laura's familiar figure. Laura groaned and moved awkwardly, her hands feeling in front of her.

'Who's there?' she demanded, her voice sounding thin and strained. 'I can't see . . . Who is that?'

'It's me, Zoë,' Zoë admitted, as Laura's eyes searched the air blankly.

'Zoë?' Laura reached out to touch at her arm. 'Zoë, I'm blind . . . Help me get up.'

Putting an arm under Laura's shoulders, Zoë managed to help her to stand and they stumbled onwards, Zoë holding the lighter ahead of them.

A little way onwards they heard voices ahead and, lifting her sightless eyes, Laura said, 'I hear Alex.'

She was right. Stumbling towards them were Alex and Jhezra, both limping and wet with blood. They stopped when they saw Zoë and the four of them stood together in silence for a moment.

'Zoë, are you injured?' Jhezra asked eventually and Zoë shook her head.

'No,' she said, ignoring her scrapes and bruises. 'But Laura's blind.'

'Oh, God.' Alex buried his head in his hands, turning away from them. 'God, no . . . This is all my fault.'

Zoë didn't contradict him.

'The mountain fell in, didn't it?' she said to Jhezra. 'We're trapped.'

'Yes,' the Hajhi girl agreed. 'These are the tunnels

beneath the city. They go on for miles but the mountain falling will have destroyed any way out. We must decide if we would rather die here or wander through the darkness until we die.'

Alex groaned again and Laura's head lifted at the sound, her face swinging round to find him. 'This is your fault,' she berated him. 'If it hadn't been for your bombs . . . '

'Enough.' Jhezra put her hand firmly on Laura's arm. 'The plan failed. Let's not spend the time that remains to us blaming each other.'

Alex turned to look at her, his expression despairing.

'It wasn't supposed to end this way,' he protested. 'We were supposed to win.'

'What makes you think that?' Zoë asked him incredulously. 'Just because you found that Door? That doesn't make you special . . . You weren't chosen by God for some great destiny. You were just lucky, that's all.'

Alex looked away and after a moment Jhezra went to his side, taking his hand in hers. Laura was silent, her blind eyes expressionless.

Zoë turned away from them. In just a week her entire world had been turned upside down and now she was standing under a mountain trapped in a room without doors, in a tunnel with no end, waiting for death or despair. She swallowed, thinking of her father, returning to their house to find her gone forever into another world. Then her heart skipped a beat suddenly as she remembered something and the tears dried in her eyes.

'It's not over yet,' she said out loud and the others stared towards her. Zoë turned to look at them. They might not be the friends she'd choose but they were all she had and she couldn't leave them here. 'It's not over,' she repeated. 'We still have a chance.'

'A chance at what?' Jhezra asked, standing ready despite her injuries. 'What is your plan, Zoë?'

'Morgan told me there was another Door,' Zoë explained. 'Buried beneath the city at the bottom of a water reservoir. If it's down here, we can find it.'

'Morgan.' Laura's face went cold and contemptuous and Zoë glared at her.

'Shut up,' she said angrily. 'What other choice have you got? Either we try and find this Door or we can curl up and die here. Which choice do *you* prefer?'

Jhezra nodded silently, her decision obvious as she straightened up, seeming to shake off her injuries.

'I'll follow you, Zoë,' she said. 'We'd die without hope as surely as we would without light and air. Whatever chance there is I'll take. Anything else is madness.'

'Madness,' Alex echoed, allowing Jhezra to lead him forward.

Laura said nothing but she allowed Zoë to take her arm, walking along passively at her side, her blind eyes staring straight ahead.

Zoë looked down the tunnel of black stone and saw no sign of light ahead. Supporting Laura on her left arm, she stepped forward into the darkness.

Outside in the desert the mountain ponies finally came to a staggering halt, shaking with their exertions, and their riders stared back at the ruin behind them.

Charm and Ciren looked back at their companions. Morgan and Kal clung together on the other pony. The boy Archon's face was white and his eyes were fixed on the destruction of Shattershard while Morgan held on to him, one hand supporting his injured sword-arm and the other wound tightly into his belt.

'What now?' Charm asked quietly, looking at her twin, and Ciren glanced up and down the road.

'We can't go back,' Morgan said out loud and her gaze shifted away from the destroyed city and down the road to a stand of rocks some distance down the desert road.

'There's nothing to go back to,' Kal said, turning his back on the ruins of the city. His hand went to the spiked crown he still wore on his head. 'What good is a crown without a city?' he asked bitterly, preparing to remove it.

Ciren's eyes flickered across at his twin and then back to Kal.

'Some use, perhaps,' he said. 'Crowns should not be so easily discarded.' His purple-black eyes met Kal's seriously. 'Keep it,' he said. 'It's all you have left.'

'You have me too,' Morgan said quickly and fiercely, her arms hugging around Kal tightly, and the twins exchanged a glance. 'What?' she asked them and they met her stare impassively.

'There's a long road ahead,' Ciren said at last. 'We should get moving.'

Charm nodded, kicking their pony as she turned its head away from the city and south-east towards the mountain road. Morgan reached round Kal to grip the reins of their own pony as it followed at a slow walk. At their back the light from the city's funeral pyre filled the sky, the smoke blocking out the stars strung out across the barren borderlands, as they took the first steps down the long dusty road.